A Chest Full of Surprises!
Five super steamy male to female stories

I was Feminized by a Demon
The Feminized Man
Super Rabbit Sex Pills
Feminization All the Way
Feminized For His Own Good

Grace Mansfield

I CHANGED MY HUSBAND INTO A WOMAN!

A delightful novel of total power exchange!

GRACE MANSFIELD

I Changed My Husband into a Woman!
Check it out at…
https://gropperpress.wordpress.com

TABLE OF CONTENTS

I was Feminized by a Demon!

Trapped in a woman's body with no way out

PART ONE

The first thing I noticed was her legs. Long stems made sexy by black high heels. Her toes were red and thet bobbed up and down, bouncing one heel by the sling. The legs went up, vicious curves that swooped up to milky thighs. Her black dress was short, just covering her panties. If she had on panties. I couldn't see any lines on her beautiful, round ass. Above that spectacular ass was a thin waist in a tight fitting sheath. Her fine flesh showed through portholes on the sides of the slinky dress, and through a heart shaped cut out over her large breasts. Large, hunh! They were torpedoes, actually looked like they were in those bullet bras from the fifties, except I couldn't see any straps. Just that deep, deep cleavage.

"Are you going to eat me with your eyeballs or buy me a drink?"

I blinked and my head jerked around. She was watching me in the mirror at the back of the bar. Her eyes were dark, smoldering, and her red lips were pursed in amusement. Her hair was done up French style, but in a sloppy manner. Wisps of her gorgeous brunette hair curled this way and that.

"Sorry," I said, sliding onto the bar stool next to her. At the end of the bar Joe was talking to some babe, with buck teeth and moles and a tendency to giggle raspily.

"Bullshit," she said.

I clinked on a glass to get Joe's attention and held up two fingers.

While Joe ambled through the process of making me a Coke High, and whatever the lady was drinking, I said, "Potty mouth." I was smiling, and so did she.

"I like the taste of soap," she murmured, then, in a whisper I almost didn't hear, "among other things."

We sat and waited for Joe, and watched each other in the mirror.

She took out her compact and freshened her lipstick. Kissed at the mirror, or me, it was hard to tell, then put her compact in a small purse.

And, for a brief second, I felt nervous, and there was a voice inside me telling me to just move on. That this one was dangerous.

But who the hell ever listens to those little voices, eh?

"Todd Lundgren," I said. And I was. And Todd Lundgren happened to be six feet tall, just let go by the Miami Dolphins, and well built. And, I wasn't overly ugly.

"You're an ugly fuck."

I blinked. Potty mouth, indeed.

She placed a hand on my forearm, it felt cool, yet it made me feel warm. "Don't mind me. I'm just pulling your dick."

I shook my head, and Joe arrived with the libations. I tilted, took a large sip, and placed the glass on the bar.

Her drink, looked like the same as mine, sat in front of her, cold and sweaty looking, a little, skinny straw poking up.

"Lady, are you for real?" Yet there was no animosity here, just a grin. I was going to get laid. I knew it in my bones.

"No. I am the most unreal thing you have ever met. Now, drink your drink. Joe, get him another one. He's going to need it."

I grinned, "And why am I going to need it?"

"Because I am going to turn you inside out and upside down. I am going to fuck you till you don't know your asshole from your chin. Furthermore, I am going to…" she leaned closer and whispered into my ear. As she poured sex into my ear I felt my cock doing the mambo in my pants.

She finished speaking. Didn't take her hand off my forearm, I guess she liked the ownership, and sipped her drink. I watched her red lips suck that little straw and my mind was about exploding.

I just came down to watch the game on the bar big screen. I hadn't intended on picking anybody up. And now…here…I gulped my drink down and Joe brought another one.

I was tipsy and she guided me to my car.

"Let me drive," and she poured me into the passenger seat. She then went around the front of the car, I watched her sexy ass bounce through the headlights, and got in behind the wheel.

"Say," I mumbled, "I don't even know your name."

"Better that way."

"You're not married, are you?"

"No," she laughed. "That's one of the conditions."

"Conditions?" I asked, "What conditions?"

"Oh, there are all sorts of conditions. You'll find out."

I was drunk, or I would have queried further. I mean, I didn't want pre-nups or bastards, I just wanted a roll in the hay. But what kind of guy is going to ask those kinds of questions when a bountiful babe is driving him him down the street and has her hand on his crotch?

I directed her to my house, a two story with a garage taking up a third of the bottom. It was pretty swank, if I do say so, and I was glad I had paid it off before I retired.

We got out of the car and walked to the gate before the stairs. When she searched for the key to the gate I pulled here around to me and kissed her.

She didn't resist, but she didn't seem too excited, either.

I pulled back and looked at her.

"Wait till we get inside, slick."

And I believed her because her hand was in my pants, roaming around and doing what hands in pants have been doing ever since pants were invented.

She found the key and I followed her up the steps. It didn't look like she had panties, and I really liked the view.

"Nice place," she said, putting her little wrist purse down and looking around.

A large living room with a big window looking out over bay. We could see the blink of lights as midnight cabin cruisers bobbed and wallowed.

She went to the window and pulled the drapes. Curious. Most chicks liked to fuck with the whole bay watching them.

"You don't want to watch the world?"

"I don't want the world to see," then she turned to me.

Now there was no reticence, now she plastered her mouth against mine, hungrily, as if trying to suck the essence right out of me.

"Fuck," I whispered as she ripped my clothes off.

"That's the idea, slick," she was on her knees now, shoving my underwear down and gobbling on my dick.

"Fuck!" I muttered, a different tone of voice, an awe in my manner, as she stroked me and slapped my balls.

She pushed me back on the couch, it's a wide one, designed for trysts like this. She stood up and pulled her slinky dress off.

Her breasts were perfect. No sag, but not fake. The nipples hard and erect like little penises. Pointing right into my mouth.

She arched her back and moaned as she held my head to her breasts.

I puckered and sucked and, man, they were delicious. I could feel the heat of her as she climbed onto my lap.

She was sitting on me now, and one hand was searching for my penis. She found it, held it, and sat on it.

I felt her warmth slide down over me, engulf me. She was incredibly tight, and it almost hurt, it was so good.

Then she hit bottom, and something funny happened. She connected. Like a switch had been clicked, and she didn't rise up. There she sat, owning me, as if our flesh was connected.

"Hey!" I blurted. I tried to rise up, to get the old in and out going, but she was content to just sit there. She put a hand on my chest and pressed.

"Wait," she said. "Let it happen."

"Let what happen?" I was starting to sober up. Something was weird. I didn't like this scene.

"Oh, baby," she whispered. She kissed me again, but it was like she was kissing me to shut me up, not out of passion.

She pulled back slightly, I could feel her warm breath, and she whispered, "Oh, baby. I'm going to fuck you. I am going to fuck you up, fuck you down, fuck you all around.

"How about getting the fuck off me?"

I tried to push up, to throw her off, but it only resulted in a pain in my groin.

"OW! What the fuck!"

"Easy, slick, it takes a little time."

"What are you...get off me!"

I managed to stand up, and it was as if she was fastened to me. I had my hands under her ass to support her, but it felt like if I let go my dick would rip off!

"Whee!" she chortled as I spun around and tried to dislodge her.

"Get off!" I growled, but it was a weak growl. In fact everything seemed to be getting weak. Suddenly my legs were weak and I couldn't support her. I started to fall forward, I frantically turned towards the couch. My arms were now too weak to carry her, and I fell forward.

She landed on the couch, her hair bounced and my dick went slamming into her depths.

"Fuck, yeah!" she grunted, the breath forced out of her.

"Please...please..." I felt myself growing ever weaker, and then I couldn't move. I was just a limp noodle, laying on top of her.

She, on the other hand, was getting stronger. Her female muscles, once no match for mine, now rolled me over and she assumed the mount position.

"What...what...?" Everything was dizzy and hazy. But it was like I couldn't pass out. Something was keeping me awake, aware, and I felt things happening to my body.

I felt like I was shrinking, and my chest, it was hurting, expanding.

But the worst thing was my groin. It felt like I was being pulled inside out by the dick. I felt like my dick was getting longer, and skinnier, and my balls...my balls hurt worse than if a place kicker kicked them over the goalposts.

"Fuck!" And now I wasn't protesting, I was just exuding the pain that was going through me.

But worse than even the worst thing, the girl was changing. Like a werewolf on one of those shitty, late night movies she was changing. Her hair retracted, was sucked right into her skull, and her head was getting big, turned more squarish, and the nose and jaw firmed up.

"Wha..." I whimpered, pushing weakly.

Then she was a man, and I felt weak and fragile, and my chest...

somebody had tied pillows to my chest and they flopped all over the place.

"Almost done, slick. And, man, it feels good."

And, finally, I felt that weird, almost clicking sensation that I had felt when I had gone balls deep…and he slid out of me.

He…slid out? Of me? WTF! WTF! WTF!

He stood up, a husky man with a day's growth on his firmly shaped face. His chest was broad and looked like a rack of nothing but muscles. Worse, however, was the big swinging dick sprouting out from his hairy groin.

"What…happened?" I got up on my elbows, and this brought my attention down to my chest. I had breasts. And further down…my dick was gone. I had…I had…a pussy!

I would have shrieked and fainted, should have shrieked and fainted, but, again, it was like there was something stopping me. Some big awareness sitting behind mine, saying, stay there, watch…watch…

The guy grinned. "Man, it feels good to be back." He looked around. "Man, this is nice. You used to play football, eh?"

"What did you do to me?" My voice was higher, girlish, and, at the moment, a little shrill.

He walked around the living room, looked at the furniture, the pictures on the wall. "Oh, yeah, here's a team picture. I remember that year. That was before I changed."

"Changed? What change?"

He opened the drapes and turned to me. "You've already done the change. You know what happened."

"But why? Why me?"

"Why not you?" He shrugged. Then: "Let's have a drink, and I'll tell you what I know, before you leave."

"Leave? I'm not leaving!"

He just smiled and went into the kitchen and began looking for the makings.

I stood up, and saw myself in the big glass window.

I was shorter, maybe five foot two. I was probably 120 pounds, and 20 of those pounds were on my chest.

And the longer I stood there the more it seemed that I was looking like…like her, who I had just fucked but…but what the fuck was happening?

"What did you do to me?" I whispered.

I had long, brunette hair. My eyes were my own, but…feminized. Softer, and, dare I say it, sexier!

And I realized that with this body I wouldn't have any trouble getting men.

Men! I didn't want men! I was a man! I was in top top shape, had money, a successful life! How could this...

He came back into the room, the ice cubes clinking in the glasses he carried. He put one on the coffee table, then sat down in my easy chair.

"Sit down. I'll tell you what happened."

"Wha...what..."

"You're in shock now. I know, 'cause I was in shock when it happened to me. But if you just sit down, take a sip, we'll have a nice, polite conversation."

"Before I leave."

"Before you leave," he nodded.

I stood there, and suddenly felt awkward. My nakedness was starting to effect me. Naked people have less power than clothed people.

I looked around.

"You can put on my dress, if it'll help." He watched me almost negligently.

"What about...I can..." I started towards my bedroom.

"Your own clothes won't fit. Believe me, you'll be glad for the dress in a while."

I didn't have any choice. I had to wear something. I put on the dress.

It didn't smell like him, like a man. It smelled like a woman, the sexy perfume of the woman I had brought here.

"Weird, eh? And it'll get a lot weirder until you embrace it, go with it."

"What did you do?" I stood in the dress. I saw myself in the window glass. Wearing clothes I was even sexier. It totally emphasized my boobs.

He sipped, sighed, and said, "I picked up a girl...what year is this?"

What year? What the fuck? I told him.

"Hunh! Three years ago. I picked up a girl, man, she was a looker. Amazing babe. Big jugs, round ass, a face to die for...sort of like the babe I was when you picked me up. Sort of like you...right now."

I stared at him.

"So I picked her up, and she did to me what I did to you. Then she kicked me out."

"But...but..."

"I don't know exactly what happened. I just know that I changed into her, she changed and became me. I was a weight lifter, world class, had endorsements and everything. I wasn't living as good as this, but I was doing okay. Then she had it all."

"But she...how could she take it? People would see that she wasn't you!"

"Do I look like you?"

And...he did! He was shifting, changing, and taking on my features.

"But...this is crazy!"

"It is, isn't it?" And he mused, "I should probably forget about weight lifting. I'm older now, and this body is built for other things. Pretty good body, eh?"

He lifted his arms and looked at them, smacked his fist into a palm a couple of times.

"But...why?"

"Like I said, I don't know. I just know that somebody changed me, and I changed you, and the guy who changed me...it looked like he was changed by somebody." He shrugged. "So your guess is as good as mine. An ancient curse? Witches? Demons? Maybe God just doesn't like us."

"But what'll happen to me?"

"You'll go fuck a bunch of guys. And, don't worry, you'll get over your revulsion and you'll start to enjoy it. And, I think this is what happens, after a while you build up a head of steam and...you change back.

"Honestly, I felt it coming. So I made sure I picked out a handsome fellow who looked well off, and..." He shrugged.

"This is not fair," I hissed. "It's evil."

"Evil spelled backwards is live. Now, if you don't mind, I'd like to be alone."

"But you can't..."

But he could. He stood up, grabbed me by the upper arm and marched me to the front door. Down the steps. Through the gate, and the gate clanked...with me on the wrong side.

I turned and looked at him. He pushed his purse, now my purse, through the bars.

He smiled. "If you try to break in I'll punch you in the nose. It'll hurt, but your body seems to heal pretty good, and then I'll call the police."

"But you...you can't...can't I live here until I...I..."

"Not a chance. You'll probably be looney for a while. I can't take a chance on fucking you, it might reverse everything, and I sure don't want to wake up some morning with my nuts in the kitchen sink."

"You fucker!" I yelled. "You son of a bitch! You can't do this to me!"

"See?" he said, and he trotted up the stairs. My stairs, to my house.

He closed the door and I stopped ranting. I stood there, wanting to scream. But, once again, it was like something was in the back of my mind, watching me watch.

I turned around. Chuck Nelson, my neighbor, was standing in his doorway, watching me.

"Can I help you, miss?"

Could he help me. Yeah, hold down the fucker who was in my house so I could have sex with him. Watch me turn into myself...maybe

11

you can fuck the girl, whichever one of us she ended up being, yourself.

I waved a hand and trudged, as well as my high heels would allow me.

And, walking down the street, I looked at my high heels. And I looked at the dress. They felt…natural, a part of me. When I had changed…had the high heels suddenly appeared? I had a feeling they would have. And I had a feeling the dress would have somehow found its way on my body.

How odd, I felt like I had a secret knowledge, a woman's intuition, if you will, about such things.

I looked at the purse dangling from my wrist. I stopped, and looked inside. A driver's license with my picture on it. Florida. Would it change to Georgia if I went to Georgia?

I had a feeling it would.

A tube of lipstick. Probably replenish itself. And I unscrewed the base and coated my lips. Naturally, as if I had been painting my lips all my life.

I knew then that I was changed on the inside. That I had feelings and knowledge that I didn't have before. Something to help me survive, no doubt. At least that was what I intuited.

I walked, and cars slowed down, no doubt to stare at my sexy ass, then continued. But it was early. I had a feeling I was going to be a magnet for assholes within a short time.

Assholes. Guys like me when I had been a man.

I walked, and marveled at how cool and sexy it was to walk in high heels. It made my ass sway, and my boobs quivered with every step.

A car came to a stop next me, "Need a ride?"

A horny, old goat. White mustache and goatee, doubtless married and anxious to get out and about.

"No thanks." Though there was a piece of me that wanted a ride. A ride on his dick.

But I hated the thought! I was revolted by the idea of a man's dick being…inserted…shoved into my…I hated the idea.

But something, way back where I was being watched, liked the idea.

Liked the idea of eyes on my caboose, lust for my mounds, an erect pecker for my…my pussy.

I kept walking. I had no destination…I was just thinking, absorbed in my tragedy.

Another car pulled up.

"Hey, senorita…I'd like to eat ya." A bunch of teenagers laughed hysterically, then the car jetted off.

Assholes. Young they were assholes, old they were assholes. Could I ever find a man that…

But I didn't want a man! I wanted my body back!

Or did I? I was feeling pretty good, the shiver of my boobs as I walked, it was exciting. And the way my ass swayed, it made me feel moist, ready.

Now how could this be? I was revolted by men, even the thought of myself as being a man, and yet…I was horny…and yet I wanted to be me again.

I felt like I was being dragged in eight different directions, and I wasn't sure what I wanted.

I had walked at least two miles, I was back near the bar I had been at, and traffic picked up.

Oddly, my feet didn't hurt. I had heard all the whining about women wearing heels for 15 minutes and then feeling like their feet were falling apart.

Heels. Dress. Nothing else. Not even any underwear. A part of me.

A car slowed down. "You all right?"

It was a pair of cops. I knew, immediately, that they thought I was a hooker. Hell, I didn't want to spend time in jail.

I leaned down to the window and gave them a full view of my cleavage. "My asshole boyfriend dumped me. I'm just walking up to that bar," I pointed at the bar I had been in earlier that night. "I'm going to call an Uber."

The cops stared at my cleavage. I let them. The longer they stared the less inclined they would be to arrest me.

Now how did I know that?

And then I knew. It was that feeling in the back of my skull. That watcher feeling. Somebody was prompting me, helping me along. I guess there wasn't much fun in watching me spend the night in jail.

No, the watching thing wanted something more from me. This watcher thing wanted to watch me have sex. It was a pervert. A filthy, fucking pervert.

Okay," the cop finally said, bringing his eyes up to me.

I walked on, and the cops sat there and watched me. Asshole men.

The name of the bar was the Wild Mustang. It was a sports bar, but the owner, Joe, hired big-titted women to wait on the tables and the place got wild at night.

I entered the Wild Mustang just as the cop car zoomed off, and walked through the short foyer and into the bar proper.

When I had been there—what, an hour ago?—men had been scarce. Just a few eating a late lunch, or an early dinner. Only a lone girl had been on the pole, and the music was low. I had been planning on having a drink, then heading into the back room to have dinner and watch the big screen TV.

A sports bar during the day, a stripper club at night. The best of both worlds.

13

I walked up to the bar, and suddenly realized I had no money. Oh, fuck! I opened up the purse and looked for something, a credit card, a fold of bills, anything.

Nothing.

"How'd it go? Did that one work?"

Joe placed a Coke High in front of me. I stared at him.

He froze, then grinned. Oh, fuck, you changed. You're the new one."

"You…how did you…"

Joe flopped a bar towel over his shoulder and leaned on the bar. He showed me his teeth. "I've seen you girls…or girl…whatever…come and go."

"You know about the change!"

"Hey, they change, they stagger in her in shock, and they talk. I know pretty much everything."

"Then why did this happen to me?"

"First, what's your name?"

"Todd! I'm Tod Lundgren!"

"Sure. I know you."

I gulped the glass down.

"It always amazes me how you girls can drink like a fish and it never effects you."

Magic," I blurted, not having any real reason. "Now tell me what is happening."

"Well," he looked around, the other two bar men had come on. He looked back at me. "You want some dinner? We can sit and talk."

"Yeah. Sure."

Funny, I was starved, I hadn't had dinner before I had been picked up—I didn't think of it as me picking up the girl—but I was just hungry. Not weak. I had a feeling I could try to starve myself to death and get nothing but hungry.

Yippee. I really was magic. So fucking what.

PART TWO

We sat in Joe's office chewing on steaks. Joe was drinking from a big bottle of Coke and I was sipping from a big bottle of bourbon. The bourbon made me feel good, but didn't give me any real drunkenness.

"Okay, so give."

"Well, here's the deal. The girl stays the same, they fuck a lot of guys, and eventually they change into them, and then thee's a new guy in the girl. If that makes sense."

Oh, baby, it made sense, all right.

"But why?"

"Nobody knows. You just fuck, some sort of mind swap or something happens, and business as usual. Speaking of which…"

"Yeah?"

"You want to keep going with our arrangement?"

"What arrangement?"

Without embarrassment or hesitation he went on. "You use my bar for your base of operations. Guys come in to see you. You're sort of like a magnet. I'll warn you off if a cop comes in, I'll send you guys who are handsome and have money. You pay me $300 a week and a fuck. Oh, and Jimmy, on the bar, he gives you free drinks, but all he wants is a fuck every week."

I stared at Joe. I had never thought he was a bad guy. He was handsome, smart, and fun to talk to. But this…this…

"I understand if you want to figure things out first. We don't have to restart our deal for a week. I know it takes you guys that long to get used to everything."

"So I'm supposed to whore for you."

"Look, don't get mad. I know you pull in at least ten grand a week. So I'm not ripping you off, just providing a service. Take your time. Free drinks while you think and…and adapt."

Okay, I could put him on hold. "Where do I usually sleep?"

That's your trailer in the back. Your key is under the third red, brick from the left in the planter box back there. That's actually what the $300 is for, parking in my lot."

I was finished with my steak. I didn't feel full, but I wasn't hungry. I had a feeling that food wasn't going to be my thing. I knew what my thing was going to be. I was already feeling an itchy, warm sort of sensation in my groin. But I didn't want to fuck men.

"Look," Joe said, putting his knife and fork down. "I'm not trying to hustle you, I've been down this road with you before, and I know how bitchy you can get. So I leave you strictly alone. The most I'll do is remind you when to pay or fuck. And sometimes you'll put me off for a while. But you always come around, and you bring in business, and, I'll admit it, you're a fine piece of ass. No offense. So you go on about your business, get used to things, and we can talk later, or whenever you want."

And we left it there.

I went out to the trailer, found the key, and let myself in.

It was a 1940 30 foot airstream Classic. And it was in primo condition. Apparently I spared no expense on making sure I was comfortable.

There was a big screen TV at one end. The bathroom was small, but modern. In one corner of the living room was a stand of plastic storage bins.

I opened up one of the storage bins and gaped. It was filled with money. Nice neat money. Stacks of twenties. Rubber banded. Tightly wrapped. I counted bills in a stack and the number of stacks in the storage bin. 100 bills in a stack, $2000. 20 stacks. $40,000. Fuck. And five bins high. An easy $200,000. And there was more money in a closet, and in a dresser. In fact, there were no clothes, just a few toiletries in the bathroom. Nothing but money.

So the guy, the girl who I was now, didn't eat, didn't wear anything but this black dress and heels, and had a never ending supply of red lipstick.

That gave me pause to think.

She probably ate at Joe's Wild Mustang. Or, hell, I hated to think this, maybe she sucked so many guys off that that was how she got her nourishment.

And outside of that, when she wasn't fucking, or sucking, what? Watch the big screen TV in the trailer? Count money?

Thinking of the money made me think of the guy who had stolen my life. He didn't care about the money in the trailer. Sure, I had lots of money, and he could no doubt learn to forge, use my credit cards, he wouldn't be hurting. but to leave a million dollars in the trailer? To just walk away?

And that made realize something: he wanted to be gone from…from this female body so bad that he just up and ran away. Fuck the money.

So his life was that miserable.

Of course, he wouldn't hurting, living off my stash, but, still…

Then I started thinking about him. I couldn't complain to the cops. I could, however, have a few home boys beat the living crap out of him.

Oddly, though that thought crossed my mind, I didn't have any real motivation in that direction.

Having him beat to a pulp would't get me my life back.

And, sitting there thinking all these thought, I became aware that my pussy was feeling...hot. Like dripping hot.

I groaned and reached a hand to my pussy.

Fuck, I was wet down there. If the black dress hadn't been black there would have been a wet spot on my dress.

I turned on the big screen TV to take my mind off my situation. I had intended to watch the Dolphins earlier, so why not now...the game was still on...but a porn channel came up.

Fuck! I started to hit the clicker, then stopped. I was caught by the bounce of flesh on the screen. A woman with big tits was getting railed by two guys. I watched, suddenly fascinated as one big dick rammed down her mouth, then withdrew as the other big dick rammed down her pussy, and back, and the other dick...and her tits were hanging down, big, enormous jugs, swaying back and forth in time to the robust fuck they were giving her.

She moaned, one hand reaching down between her legs and feeling the rear man's balls. The other hand was reaching up to grab the front man's balls.

The guys moaned. They pumped in and out. They slapped her ass and pulled her hair, and she loved it.

I adjust my position, and suddenly found that my dress had ridden up and my hand was down there...exploring.

How many times had I done this to a woman, used my hands and fingers to get her off? And now I was doing it to myself.

I felt my labia, ran a finger up the slit and shivered. On the screen the men flipped the woman over. One man sat down and the woman sat on him. Facing him. The other man moved up behind her and aimed for her asshole.

I had my fingers in my snatch now, and I was exploring, experiencing all the sensations I gave women, but now was giving myself. I was moaning, my mouth was open, and I started drooling. Actually drooling.

"Oh, baby," one of the men said.

"Ride my rocket," blurted the other one.

The woman groaned and writhed and said, "I need more. Give me more."

My fingers were in me, my skull was on fire. I felt white heat coming for me, welling up out of some secret sex pit in my body, then it burst over me. I orgasmed with a drawn out sort of yelp.

On the screen the woman yelled that she was cumming. The men were grunting like broken trains.

I laid back and tried to control my breathing.

More fucking sounds filled the little trailer. I grabbed the clicker and turned the TV off.

And lay there.

And…was horny.

Fuck! I had just cum! I didn't need to cum again!

But I did.

I stood up, straightened my dress. I got up and went for a glass of water. I opened the cupboards and…more money. fuck! I almost didn't want to see any more money!

I held my hair back and drank from the faucet. I straightened up, wiped my mouth. I turned around and leaned my butt against the sink. To one side was a little drawer. Not thinking, I opened it.

Bank books. And the accounts were filled with money. There were numbers on the books, so I knew I could simply get on a computer and transfer money. Which was good because the books had different names.

Sheila Bester. Tina Walkson. Annie Garret. Alyce Thorndyke. And on and on and on.

How many women had worn this body?

And, heysoos, the last one had REALLY wanted to get out of it.

Tell the truth, just thinking about it was making me want to get out of it.

In my male body I went and had a few drinks with friends, met an occasional lady, and had a good time.

In this body I was…I could feel it…I was committed to sex.

I was horny all the time, a growing, gnawing horniness. And jacking off, pardon me, jilling off, didn't cut it.

Restless, I stomped out of the trailer, locked the door, and put the key under the brick.

I went to the back entrance of the Wild Mustang and entered.

The place was in full roar now. Hundreds of horny men swaggered around, packed the area in front of the stage with the pole on it.

A girl twirling around the pole waved at me and I waved back. I guess I knew her.

The bartender saw me. He popped a drink down in front of me. His nameplate said, 'Jimmy.'

I raised a hand in thanks and picked it up and drank a couple of big gulps.

Jimmy was off pouring beers and mixing drinks, so I slowed down and watched the crowd.

Men whooping as the girl on the pole flashed her boobs. Men laughing and telling raucous jokes. Men, with their hands in their pockets, wearing tight jeans and swaggering about like they had big dicks.

Asshole men. And my pussy physically hurt for sex.

I sauntered through the crowd, searching the faces.

Kids. Old men. Drunks. Guys looking for fights. Guys conversing importantly.

Bing! A guy caught my eye.

He was wearing an expensive suit, looking at his wristwatch. I started towards him and felt a hand on my shoulder. I turned, and Joe mouthed, 'cop.'

I nodded, and went in another direction. My eyes searching the crowd, my hot vagina forcing me on. I needed...I needed... some relief down there. My reluctance to be with a man faded in the face of this compulsion.

I went back to the bar, and Jimmy placed another drink in front of me and grinned.

I was going to have to fuck Jimmy.

Well, okay. He wasn't ugly. But, Geez, he was paying for my pussy with Joe's liquor.

Oh, well. No skin off my back.

"This seat taken?"

I turned, and my heart stopped. He was a few inches taller than me, handsome as all get out, and obviously had money. He oozed of money.

I looked past him to Joe, who gave me a thumbs up. Okay. Joe approved. Not a cop.

"Take a load off," I sighed, actually relieved that a man had come to me.

"Name's Emmet."

"I'm me," I said, my pussy twitching uncontrollably. "Do you want to bother with small talk or get right down to it?"

His mouth opened slightly and he blinked. "Maybe I could get a drink first?" He was disconcerted, but he wasn't leaving. Good. God, I needed my hole filled with man meat. And this guy would do till the next one came alone.

I waved to Jimmy and quickly the order was filled.

"Well, Me," he said, as he sipped, "How are you doing?"

"I am so fucking horny I can't believe it. And I'm wet down there. I didn't know a girl could get so wet. Are you still drinking? Come on!"

I grabbed his hand. I couldn't wait to get him out of there. I needed him in me.

He allowed himself to be pulled, sucking his drink down and placing it on a passing table. Then we were out the door.

"You got a car?"

"Over—"

I jerked him in the direction his head had started to turn in.

He drove a Tesla.

"Heysoos forked a dork," I whispered. "An electric car for an electric fuck. Shall we just do it here?"

"I…uh…"

I scrambled into the car, laid over the front seat and pulled my dress up.

I can only imagine what he was thinking. Running into a nympho maniac. Being dragged out to his expensive car and fucked like a teenager.

But, whatever he was thinking, it was heaven when I felt his body lean on mine, and his dick poked against my thighs.

I edged up a little, gave him more access, then he plugged me. Stuffed his fat sausage right into my little pleasure palace and wiggled it.

Oh, God, it felt so good. It felt like heaven, and yet…there was something wrong. And I immediately knew what it was. That watcher thing. I felt like I was being shoved aside and whatever, whoever, was watching me was taking my place, accepting the dick that I wanted, getting his jollies off the act that I had earned and instigated and craved.

I was still there, I could move my arms and legs, I could twist my hips and push back and I could feel that cock splitting me in two. I could feel the hands groping my fine tits.

But somebody else was feeling the thrill.

"Fuck," I whispered, and I almost wanted to cry.

So this was why the other girls had wanted to get out of this body. Or…or…they had been turned in! For a new model.

Whatever it was that watched wanted to experience new sensations, new reluctance, new horniness, new shivers of excitement and disgust.

So fuck a few hundreds times, it got tired, and…zingo bingo, I was the new model.

I lay there, getting nothing out of the fuck, and I knew that I would come out of this damned Tesla as horny as I went in.

And the money…it wasn't mine…it belonged to the thing that watched, that yelped and screamed in my mind.

No wonder the other girls didn't want it. They didn't want to be reminded of all the times they had fucked…and been robbed.

It must have felt like somebody was manipulating their lives and sucking the sap right out of their soul.

I suddenly didn't blame the asshole who had given me this body.

But, no matter what I felt, Emmet what'shisname was fine with the arrangement. In fact, he acted like it was the best fuck in his life.

I stood there and he took out his wallet and shoved twenties in my hands.

"Thank you. Thank you." He bubbled. "That was incredible."

I took the money and held it in my mitts as he wheeled out of the parking lot. Semen was running down my legs and splattering on my heels.

I went back into the bar, placed all the money in the tip jar on the bar and headed for the girl's room. I noticed Joe watching from the side, a sad expression on his face. How many women had he seen act like this, fuck and end up with self loathing and self hate. I had only seen one, and it was already too much.

The girl's room, it was labeled 'Fillies,' was filthy. Not because it was that kind of bar, but because it had seen so much action.

I went into the stall and wiped the gizz off my legs. Tears dropped on my thighs and I used that to help wash myself.

"Come on, baby!" The door banged open and a couple barged in. They couldn't see me in the stall, and they locked the door and he hoisted her up on the sink. She giggled and wiggled out of her panties.

"Ooh," she gasped. "You're so big…"

I watched through a crack in the door their reflections in a mirror.

He stood between her legs, shoving his hips forward.

She held on to him, clung to him, and they fucked mindlessly, joyfully, and without some hidden creature watching from inside their minds.

They were drunk, probably just getting a quickie, but I envied them. I envied their…aloneness. Just them, no other, porking away. Pretending their lust was love…but that was okay. Anything was better than what I had experienced.

I was being whored out by something that made me sexy and resilient and horny, then I was being tossed aside and ignored, and my love, even if it was just lust, was betrayed.

Fuck. As they groaned and grunted a couple of feet from me I cried silent tears.

Finally, they finished. I dried my eyes, and left the bathroom. And my induced sexuality was already coming to the fore. My eyes were sparkling, in spite of how I felt on the inside. My body absorbed lipstick smeared outside the lines, my eyes looked like they were naturally mascaraed and shadowed.

I was on the hunt again.

I stepped up to the bar and Joe poured me a drink. He handed it to me, touched my hand for a moment.

"I know how tough it is the first time, and I'm sorry. I tried to talk it up all cheerful, but I know what you're going through. If you need to talk, later, no sex or nothin', I'll be around."

I nodded, stifled a sniff, and thanked him, then I turned to the big room.

Flesh. Men with bulges in their pants. Women laughing shrilly.

Normally I would have judged it to be a party, and it probably still was, but my frame of mind…it was a dirge. A screaming clown factory. A terrible place with mattresses on the walls and dicks in all the glasses.

I wandered on to the floor.

"Hey, baby."

I danced with a tall fellow who wanted more, but wasn't up to my standards, which is to say he didn't interest the demon within.

Demon. That's what it was. I was in a demon body.

But it wasn't, really. And I didn't know what it was.

I didn't know what was driving me, nor how, nor how to stop it.

I just felt the urge grinding away at my groin, and I had to forcefully stop myself from grinding my pussy into the fellow I was dancing with.

He wanted to dance some more, but I sadly pushed him away, a bright smile on my face, as if I was prick teasing.

Another fellow wanted to dance. I walked away.

"Want to dance?"

He was six foot, but slender. Not weak, he was one of those wiry ones. But he didn't look rich. But he did.

Was he dressing down?

"What kind of car do you drive?" asked a voice that watched from behind and put the words into my mouth.

He blinked a slow blink, then, Maserati."

I nodded, and stepped into his arms.

We danced, and I felt the heat growing in my crotch. I ground my pelvis into his and felt his big boner.

"Come on," I said, halfway through the dance.

I led him towards the front door.

Joe watching. A sad look on his face.

Joe.

Joe was in love.

Of course.

How often had he fucked this body?

How often had he seen his desire go out the door with another?

Many different people, but the same body, and the same terrible tragedy roiling inside.

He was compassionate. He ran a damned bar and he felt for other people. What a guy.

Then I exited the front door and pulled the man I had picked out and headed for the parking lot.

The Maserati was a dream. Handled like a race car, accelerated nicely, and my target attempted small talk.

"My name is Charley," he said, as he shifted down for a traffic light.

Alyce," I answered, choosing one of the names I had seen on a bank book. Sounded slutty enough for the way I felt.

"Nice name," he commented.

"Thanks."

I turned to him. He was just a guy, looking for a good time. And he was about to get the fuck of his life. I knew that, though I would be relegated to the role of a watcher in my own body, and the watcher would be getting the real thrill, Charley was going to be shortly screaming in ecstasy.

"Do you pick up girls often?"

He suddenly looked uncomfortable.

Shit. I suddenly felt sorry for him. He had a compulsion, he needed love. Maybe he was a local, maybe he was a sailor in a strange port, but he just needed what we all need, and what I wasn't going to be getting. Love.

No, there might not be a lot of love in lust, but it was enough to keep us going, to keep us hoping.

"So this is a cool car!" I blurted cheerfully, and he relaxed and smiled. Let me be the airhead. So much mean was being done to me that I didn't want to do any mean to anybody else.

"I paid almost. a $100,000 for this baby." He spoke proudly, as he had given birth to it himself.

"Wow! What a lot of money! You must be rich!"

Oh, the self satisfied chuckle. I had twice what he had in my trailer alone, and probably millions in bank accounts.

"Well, I got lucky in the stock market." False humility is so endearing. Not.

He took me to the Hyatt and we walked up to his room. Now he was silent, proud of the girl on his arm, but a little ashamed, too. After all, I was...what was I? A hooker? A whore? Whatever, he would end up so totally fucked he threw money at me. But my drawers and cabinets were full of money, I didn't want money.

And I finally started thinking.

So many people get problems but don't want to think about them.

Oh, I'll ignore it and maybe it will go away.

That wasn't my modus operandi in life, and certainly wasn't that in this new body.

So we entered his room, I turned to him and we began to kiss. Long, lush, juicy melding of mouths. Tongues twining and the heat growing, and I began to get shoved out.

Whatever was possessing me was doing the shoving, but I didn't get all upset now. Now I watched, and I thought. I observed, and hoped I would see something, anything, that would get me out of this mess.

He put me on the bed, I was a little girl and he was a big man, and he lifted me up and laid me out. He started to take off my shoes, and I blurted, "No."

He blinked, shrugged, and I pulled up my dress and gave him access.

He lay on top of me, fit his penis to my hole, and pushed.

"Oh, fuck!" He blurted, as I began to go to work. My pussy rippled and rustled. I held his cock with my vagina and overpowered it. I humped and pumped, and he began to groan in happiness.

"Fuck!" He kept whispering.

I watched from a distance.

Something else was fucking him. I was along as baggage, a spare tire.

My hips rolled and writhed, went up and down. I wrung his cock out, and he began to cry out as the orgasm hit him.

"Fuck!...Fuck!...Fuck..." An endless ejaculation of the phrase, followed by a heaping helping of baby batter.

Then he was done. Sobbing. Unable to understand what had happened.

I came back into my body. I sat up. He lay there, unable to move. He had been totally fucked out.

I went into the bathroom and washed his slime out.

I went back into the bedroom. "Take me back."

"Oh...my...I...can I call you an Uber?"

"Sure."

He got up, made a call, then dug through his wallet. He had a lot of money in there, and he wanted to give it all to me.

I took a fistful, pushed the rest away, and walked out the door.

He sat on the bed, staring after me, wondering what the hell had just happened.

I knew what happened. I had been used. And I had an idea. I had seen something, and...and maybe...

The Uber took me back to the Wild Mustang, and the whole time I sat in the corner of the rear seat and thought.

"How's the night?" asked the Uber driver.

I ignored him.

"Nice perfume you have on."

That wasn't perfume, that was my inspired body aroma. Whatever was using me to fuck made me smell like that, a natural pheromone to draw in the suckers. Pardon me, the fuckers.

I walked into the Wild Mustang, and I was immediately in the thick of things.

Frenzied, drunken masses, coupling desperately, looking for lov ein all the wrong places.

I went to Joe's office and sat down. My pussy was burning. It was on fire. I wanted more.

Joe came in, I was bent over, holding my fist to my snatch and crying.

"Are you okay?" Yet I knew that he knew what was going on.

24

"I don't want to fuck anymore."

"I know." He poured me a drink, put it in my hand. "I know."

I looked up at him, "Joe, will you help me?"

"Sure."

"I'm going to…I need to…later tonight I'll tell you."

He left, and I grabbed the bottle he had poured my drink from and glugged.

Cool liquid stoked a hot fire in my gut, and I glugged some more. I wouldn't get drunk, but I would get happy, and my mind would be off my problems for a short while, at least until whatever it was that was in me burned out the alcohol.

And, while my hand held the bottle high, while the fiery liquid gurgled down my throat, I wrote a message. There was a blank tablet on Joe's desk. There was a pen, and I wrote without seeing.

The thing in me that watched, that bullied me and made me do things let me drink. It didn't mind the drinking. It could fix the drinking.

But, my eyes closed and my head tilted upward, it didn't see what I wrote.

I swiveled the chair and got up. I put the bottle down without looking at Joe's desk. I walked out of the room.

That was the worst night of my life.

I didn't want to fuck, and whatever it was that was in me turned up the heat. My crotch was on fire, my pussy was burning. I had an urge to fuck like you wouldn't believe.

Yet I withheld myself. I walked through the bar, through the mass of drunken celebrators, and out to my trailer.

'My trailer,' I thought. 'Not his!' Whatever 'his' was.

I turned on the TV. I turned off the porn and watched a game. I don't know what game, but I watched, and I drank, and I fended off the desire to get back into that bar and fuck another man.

I wound up on the floor, rolling over, crying as my hand punched my groin. I didn't want to fuck…I didn't want to fuck…I didn't want to…

Two hours later Joe knocked on the door. Jimmy was with him.

I opened the door and launched myself at him.

"Fuck me!" I snarled. "I need a fuck!"

But he had read my note.

"Jimmy!" He called out, because I was swarming him, winning the battle for sex. I had my hand almost into his pants and Jimmy grabbed me and pulled me off.

I turned to Jimmy and tried to bite him, to kiss him, to get my lips on his dick.

Joe snatched at my dress, he began pulling it off.

25

Then I began struggling. I wanted to keep that dress on. And the shoes…I needed them on!

But he got the dress off. Jimmy held me tightly, used his whole body weight.

Joe threw the dress to one side and Jimmy managed to get me down on the ground. He used his body weight and kept me pressed flat.

Joe pulled at my high heels. He grabbed them, he was a big, strong man, and he pulled.

For a long minute it felt like the shoes wouldn't leave my feet It felt like the skin had been fused to my very soles, then one popped off.

I screamed in rage and frustration.

He pulled the other shoe off.

I tried to kick, to get loose, to do something.

Slowly, as the other shoe began to come loose, to 'de-fuse' from my flesh, I felt myself being pushed back. Away from the struggle. Then I was watching, watching as if from afar, and the other shoe popped off.

I watched myself ranting and raving like an insane asylum patient. I clawed at the ground, shredding my nails, and tried to crawl after Joe.

Joe picked up my dress and shoes and ran into the bar.

I crawled, inhuman strength, Jimmy trying to hold me back, using all his weight and strength.

I made it into the back of the kitchen.

Joe opened an oven and threw my garments into it. He turned the dial and I heard the fire go 'whooosh!'

I screamed and clawed and pounded on the earth. I made dire insult, promised to kill anybody and everybody. My voice turned hoarse and guttural.

Joe watched me, and I felt it start to leave.

That which watched was being consumed in the oven.

The clothes which had bound me as a slave turned to flame, and that which had occupied the clothes turned into a wisp.

My screams became less.

The clothes burned more, and a foul, oily smell filled the kitchen.

I stopped screaming.

Jimmy managed to get fully on top of me.

I lay, naked, under him, and sobbed, and somewhere in there the sobs turned from rage to gratitude.

I lay, and cried, and Jimmy realized I wasn't trying to hurt him or get away anymore.

"You can get off her," Joe said.

He got off, and I came to a sitting position. I hugged my knees and sobbed as if the world would end.

And, in a way, it had.

26

EPILOGUE

Whatever it was that was watching me, manipulating me, and a string of men before me for who knows how long, was in the heels and the dress.

What was it? Exactly? I don't know.

A demon? A devil? A Djinn? Who knows.

But whatever it was, when the oven flames burned the dress and high heels the thing, whatever it was, had nothing to hold on to, and it couldn't stay in this world.

And it couldn't hold on to me any longer.

I was free.

I was still a woman, but that was okay. There's nothing bad about being a woman. It's what you do as a woman that's good or bad.

I stayed in the trailer and played with money. I made deposits, shifted accounts, and eventually had over ten million dollars all to myself.

More than what I had made playing football.

And I visited my old house. Went right up to the gate and rang the bell. The guy who had started me down this path came out to the door and looked down, then he descended the stairs and faced me.

"I figured it out. I'm free now. I got free."

"I felt something," he said. "Months ago, and it felt like somebody had lifted a yoke."

"It was in the clothes, and I burned them."

He nodded. "Well, thank you." Then: "I'm sorry. I'm not going to give you back your money and house and all, but I'm sorry."

"It's okay. The money in the trailer."

"Oh, yeah," and his eyes started to marvel.

We parted on good terms, and agreed to walk across the street if we ever saw each other again.

Not because we hated each other, but because we reminded each other of that terrible blot of blackness in our lives. That thing that made us fuck mindlessly, and stole our souls.

So I was free.

And rich.

And, better, I was in love.

Joe had saved me. He had followed the directions I had written on the note. He had burned the clothes.

Sweet, compassionate Joe, who understood what the people in this body of mine had been going through.

Who could not fall in love with a man that compassionate?

And Jimmy, he looks at me every once in a while, and I know what he's thinking. He's thinking that I was the best piece of ass in the universe, and that he was not going to get to tap me any more.

Hah!

END

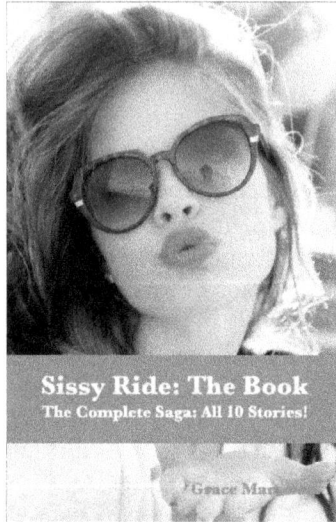

Sissy Ride: The Book!
A giant saga of feminization!
Check it out at…
https://gropperpress.wordpress.com

The Feminized Man
He is maid to serve!

PART ONE

"Honey, I just pulled in the greatest job in the world."

I stared at my wife. Look, I love her, but sometimes she comes up with crazy ideas. Like the time she tried to start a business that…well… she introduced a low current to furry dogs that was supposed to make their hair stand on end. The idea was that she could then clip their fur easier.

Unfortunately, it just made the dogs pee.

Then there was the time she was going to combine dog food with grass trimmings to make the ultimate superfood.

She tried it out on me and I had the ultimate runs for a week.

So, I love her, she's gorgeous, and she's smart in her own way, but sometimes she just gets these crazy ideas that were better left unthought.

"What job is this?"

We were sitting in our house and I was going over spread sheets. Good money in spread sheets.

"I saw an advertisement on youtube and I answered it."

"Youtube, eh?" Yikes!

"Yes, Isn't Youtube wonderful? The whole internet is wonderful. There are so many great ideas on the internet.

At that point I probably should have let her go on about the greatness of the internet. She might distracted herself and gone off on some new tangent. Instead, like a fool (I was working on those spreadsheets) I said, "Okay, give me a quick rundown so I can get back to work."

"Well," she plopped down on the sofa across from me. I was sitting on an ottoman and the spreadsheets were spread out on the coffee table. I looked over the paper and blinked.

She was naked.

Oh, man. I was trying to work and she was naked.

"I was slurfing the net…"

"Surfing the net," I offered.

"Yeah, that, slurfing, and I came across this stuff called ASMR. And right below it was the advertisement."

She was sitting naked, her legs crossed Indian style, which gave me a full view of…of…

"Are listening to me?"

"Oh, yeah," I raised my eyes to her chest. Oh, fuck. My wife has the nicest set of boobs in the world. Big and pointy, the nipples are always erect.

"Up here, bozo, this is important."

I lifted my eyeballs to her sweet face, and almost fainted. She was made up, and I loved it when her eyes were all smokey and her lips were plump and red and moist and juicy and...you get the idea.

"Yeah, LSPD."

"No, silly, ASMR."

"Oh, of course. It just slipped my mind." I licked my lips. That's just how my wife effects me. She gets nekkid and then I have an involuntary response of the tale wagging variety but it's in my crotch and not on top of my ass and then I want to...

"ASMR stands for Autonomous Sensory Meridian Response. It's the latest rage. People get on the internet and they whisper and they make sounds like it's raining or the wind blowing and it sounds so cool and then people relax and get better."

"Get better?"

"Yes, aren't you listening?"

"But get better from what? I mean, do they have dread diseases or something?"

"No, no. Nothing like that." She frowned, licked her red lips, which made my pants very uncomfortable. "It's more like if people have trouble sleeping, then they can sleep. Or if they have anxiety then they can get....I don't know, unanxious?"

"So it has a calming effect!"

"Yes!" She said brightly, clapping her hands.

"And you want to do this, this SDFG thing."

"Exactly, she gave a little bounce, which became a big bounce on her chest, and I started folding up spread sheets. I was about to have an emergency of the trousers. Mainly, I needed to take them off and...

"So I don't need much equipment, but I might need some help with things like my wardrobe."

Uh oh. My shopaholic wife was going to go shopping. I was about to have an emergency of the insufficient wallet kind.

So I cleared the spreadsheets off the table and came around and sat on the table and and asked her how much.

Little lines appeared on her forehead. "Well, I don't know exactly, yet. I'm going to talk to a woman at ASMR, Inc. today. He'll tell me what I need."

"So you want unlimited funds so you can dress right so you can whisper to people and make them relax." I said, slipping my pants off, then my underwear. I was now sitting on the coffee table and pointing at her. And I think you know what I was using for a pointer.

"Exactly!" She bounced again and I almost fainted.

"Well," I said, sagely, "I can commit to waiting until you know how much, I guess."

She blinked and turned her head slightly to the side. "I don't…"

"Honey, congratulations on your new job. I think you're going to do wonderful. The world is in better hands already."

"Really?"

"Really." I moved over to the couch and sat next to her. I put my hand on her knee and eyed her breasts.

She was ecstatic. Wiggling all around, all excited, and she hugged me.

"Oh, thank you."

"Think nothing of it," I said, lowering my head to her breasts.

She clasped my head and pulled it down and I began sucking on her nipples.

"Oh! Oh! I am so happy!"

"Me, too." I gargled over a mouthful of tit.

"I'm going to make so much money, and the world is going to be so relaxed…"

I pushed her back on the couch. She went with me, holding my head, and I managed to keep sucking her nipples. Pulling them with my teeth, licking them, making them more and more erect.

"Ooh, that feels good," she blurted, suddenly noticing what I was doing.

I put one hand on her pussy and searched for her hole.

"Right here, baby," she muttered, helping me get my hand just right, and I inserted several fingers into her snatch and began hooking and rubbing.

"Oh, yeah," I said. My boner was pressed up against one of her legs and my mouth went up to hers. I pressed my lips onto hers and she groaned and tilted her pelvic to help my hands invade her pussy.

She reached down and grabbed my pecker.

"Easy, girl."

She giggled and fit me to her. I brought my hands up to her tits and my dick began sliding into her love canal.

"Oh," she gasped.

"P," I responded.

She stopped moving and looked at me. "You always say P. Why do you say that?"

"You said O," I grunted and pulled out, "the next letter is P," I groaned and pushed in, "after that is Q. Go-o-od is that good!" I pulled out slowly, "You want to say Q?" I pushed in. "Uhuhuh!"

She giggled, and moaned, and said, "You're so smart!"

"Uhhh…yeah…" I agreed as I pulled outward again.

"Ooh…ooh!" She moaned.

"Wh-a-a-at?" I asked as I swirled my hips and drove in as hard I

could, the tip of my dick scouring her innards, and it was driving me cra-
a-azy.

"I'm going to…I'm going to…AHHHHH!"

That's the thing about Misty, she cums quicker and faster than any woman I have ever met. And sometimes it leaves me high and dry.

"Oh, yes," she purred, and she collapsed, went slack, and she pulled her hips back and I fell out. Stiff and hard and almost there…I was out.

"Uh, honey?" I tried to scoot back in, thrusting my hips and edging up on my knees.

"What? Oh, you poor boy. Well, maybe next time."

She hopped up and went to make her plans to conquer the world with ASMR.

I turned over and lay there, my dick looking like a rocket about to take off.

Crap.

Most couples have the problem of the man cumming too fast and leaving the woman high and dry. With us it's just the opposite. She has her orgasm and then it's all done, and I'm…left.

Left to wander through life with a tent in my pants and an urge that is distracting to say the least.

Which is weird. Because I'm distracted, and to take my mind off my horniness I work harder, and then I get more work done, and make more money.

But I'd rather be broke.

I got up and headed for the shower. Maybe I could get together with Madam Palm and her five daughters. Maybe—

"And don't you go playing with yourself," Misty called from the kitchen.

Fuck! Busted before I could even try.

So I went to the shower, turned it on cold for a while, and let my amorousness slip away.

And dressed and got ready for work and headed for the kitchen.

"How's my big, strong man?" cooed Misty, kissing my cheek.

"Fine," I grumped.

She patted my crotch then, and I groaned.

She giggled. "I like it when you are horny."

"You have a lot to like then, because I'm a lot horny."

She giggled again and put out my breakfast.

A hard boiled egg. A piece of bacon. A single piece of toast. Gah.

"Can I—"

"No more for you, baby. You're on a diet."

"But I don't want to be on a diet!"

She ignored me and quipped, "We have to watch your girlish figure."

"I'm already too skinny!"

"Nonsense. One can't be too skinny. Look at me!"

She was wearing just a negligee now. Under it her body was a rail, but she was a well endowed girl.

She held up her breasts and complained, "I'm just a fat cow!"

Oh...my...fucking...my boner sprang up again.

"Oh, fuck," I whined, putting my hand over my crotch.

She giggled. "I see that. You've got a boner."

She came and kissed me again, pressed that stacked body against mine and near swallowed my mouth, then she backed off and smiled, "I like it when you're hard. It shows me that you love me."

"Then I must love you a lot..." I picked up the one piece of bacon and headed for the garage.

"Honey! Your breakfast!"

"It's okay," I kissed her cheek as I passed her, "I'm on a diet." Then I was out the door and on my way to work.

I stopped on the way to work for a bag of donuts.

I worked really hard that day. I really needed to forget about my pants. I forgot all about Misty and her job, and I was pleasantly surprised when I got home.

"Honey! I got the job!"

"You did? That's wonderful. How much are they going to pay you."

"'Oh," frown, little lines between her eyes. "I'm not sure."

"You're not?" I hung up my jacket and turned to her.

She was wearing clothes. Damn. Sometimes I get home and she's not. I sighed.

"No. They were going to pay me a salary, but then they had me do the audition and they offered me my own channel."

"What? Really?"

"Is that good?"

"Well, I don't know. I mean, if you get your own channel I think it's good, but...but I would think there would be a guarantee of some kind."

"Oh."

"So when do you start?"

"I started. I went to work right after the audition. I did ASMR for two hours. I just got home."

"Oh."

"Would you like to see it?"

"Well, uh..." see my wife whisper like the rain? Or snow falling? Or some such? It sounded about as exciting as watching paint dry. Besides, I watch my wife every day.

"Oh, you don't want to. Well, I guess ASMR is not for everybody."

She flounced away. Not exactly mad, but not happy. Crap. There went my opportunity to get rid of my boner. Now that I was off work and in the presence of my sexy wife my boner was back. And bonier than ever.

So we had dinner, and watched TV, then she wanted to try out a script on me.

"A script?"

"Sure. I've got my own channel, and I have my own script."

"But...I thought you just whispered and went 'woooOOOooo,'" I made a sound like the wind.

She laughed.

"Oh, you silly! That's for the beginners."

"Well...uh, it is? What do the more advanced ASMR people do?"

"If you'd watched my channel you'd know."

"Well, let's watch it."

"It's getting late, and I need to practice my script on you."

"Oh. Okay."

We went into the living room and she had me sit on the couch. She sat across from me in the easy chair. She took off her clothes.

"What are you doing?" I asked.

"Silly, I'm putting on my work uniform."

"Your work uniform?" My voice squeaked a little.

"Sure. Everybody has a work uniform."

"Does everybody's work uniform look like yours?"

"Gosh, no. I'm the star, so I have a special uniform."

She sat before me in all her nekkid glory. Nothing but her bare flesh. Her enormous globes pointing at me. Sitting Indian style and giving me a mouth watering view of...you know.

I was blinking, trying to figure this out, and she picked up her script and began reading.

"Puuuuleeeeeeze fuuuuck meeee! IIIII ammmm hoooornnnny. IIIII waaaant toooo suuuck yooooour coooock."

My jaw dropped.

"Wait! What?"

"Oh, you made me lose my place. I'll start again. Puuuuleeeeeeze fuuuuck meeee!"

"Wait! Wait!" I rubbed my face and looked down. I looked up. "And this is what you say?"

"Oh, I say all sorts of things. This is just one script. I have lots of scripts. Want to hear another script?"

"Uh, sure," I was flabbergasted, not sure what to say.

"IIIII neeeeed iiiit uuuuup myyyyy aaaaasssssshoooole. Giiiive meeeee yooooour coooock!"

"Okay, okay," I put my hand up.

She looked at me quizzically, "What's wrong?"

"They have you say that stuff? And you're naked?"

"Well, of course! Don't you like it when I say I want to suck your cock? Or fuck? And I'm nude?" She started giggling. "You wouldn't like it if I was wearing clothes when I said those things."

"Well, uh…I don't…" the problem was…she was right!

"But, honey, this is not you and me! This is you and…and total strangers out on the net!"

"But that's the fun part! I get to talk dirty and make everybody all horny and they never actually see…uh, meet me."

"Well, yeah, but…"

We didn't get much scripting done then. We had a looooong talk about her job. And I lost.

How could I lose, you ask? How could I fail to enforce morality and decency and all that stuff.

Because, towards the end she took off her clothes.

I don't know why you're so upset," she said, as she unbuttoned her blouse. My eyes focused down.

"It's not like I'm really out there fucking anybody…" she undid her bra. I was gone at that point. I gave up talking for licking my lips.

"If I was letting somebody put their penis in my vagina I could understand," she slithered out of her pants. Or if I was actually putting my mouth around their cocks…" there went the panties. "I just want you to be more understanding."

"I'm understanding," I wheezed.

"You don't look like it. You look all upset and everything, and just because I'm going to bring home money."

"Honey, it's not that…"

"Well, come over here and tell me what it is…"

I started to rise and she held a hand out.

"No. You're being so unreasonable that I don't want to."

"What?" I squeaked.

She folded her arms, which just made her chest bounce, and looked away from me, to the side. "No. If you're going to be this way then I'm not going to make love to you."

"Honey, please." I was falling forward, on my knees, and pulling my shirt apart.

She giggled. "You did it."

"What?"

"You said, 'puuuuleeeeze.' Just like I do."

"But I…but…"

"Well," she said, getting to her feet. I was still on my knees and she looked down on me. "I've got a long day tomorrow. I still didn't memorize the script. Maybe i can get up early tomorrow and…" she continued on with her thoughts.

She had to memorize the script? All she had to do was whisper obscenities, and what did it matter what order she whispered it in?

"...so let's go to bed. I'm not going to make love, I'm a little tired, but we can cuddle. Can't we?"

"We...what...I..."

She patted my cheek and led the way to the bedroom.

I followed, dumbstruck, my cock hurting in my pants.

I didn't get much sleep that night. Of course not, I was too horny. So I got up at about two in the morning and went to the computer. I fired it up and searched for Misty.

Nothing. Of course not. Nobody would know who Misty Johnson was. I chuckled at my silliness. Nobody knew who she was and nobody would see her and that was that.

I gave a big sigh of relief.

Then I decided to find out more about this ASMR thing.

I checked it out on the net. Soft, whispering sounds, like rain, or leaves falling, or something. Huh. No big deal. Relieved stress, relaxed people. Okay.

I sat and mused. No big deal.

Still, they were asking her to do it naked.

I expanded my search to include ASMR and sex.

Bingo: 'The feeling isn't usually sexual. Although some people are triggered by videos that appear sexual...'

So that's why they wanted her to wear no clothes. Not the whispering, but the naked flesh. That's what they were looking for... visual stimulation.

And I knew that Misty was about as visually stimulating as they got.

Still, nobody know. So what if a few freaks got a look at my wife's boobs. There are worse things...I meandered my thoughts along, and absently put in ASMR in the youtube search engine. Might just as well see what this crap looks like...MISTY JOHNSON!

Fuck! The very first listing in the ASMR category was my wife!

But her tits were blurred out.

Good, no tits allowed. Good...oh, you have to sign up for the adult channel.

I clicked the box that certified I was an adult.

My eyes bulged and my cock went SPROING!

Misty Johnson, my wife, stared out from the big computer screen, took up the big computer screen In fact you couldn't see the computer screen, all you could see was her!

Her face was gorgeous, with red, red lipstick and shadowy eyes, her breasts filled the lower portion of the screen. Her nipples were obviously rigid. And she spoke:

"Puuuuleeeeze suuuuck myyyy puuuuussssssyyyy. Puuuuleeeeze fuuuuck meeeee! IIIII neeeed yoooour coooock innnn myyyy vaaaaagiiiinaaaaa!"

I stared, helpless, and…instantly enraptured.

Well, of course I was. I hadn't cum for a few days, and she had gotten off on my dick and left me high and dry, and…and here she was. Talking dirty to me, and…and she just pulled her nipple! And fondled her chest! What the…oh, my God!

But my hand was in my groin, stroking.

And she was whispering, sometimes I couldn't tell what she was saying, but her lips were moving, and it was like I was getting the world's biggest blow job, and even though I am a slow cummer, I was getting close. I was starting to feel it. I could feel the switch in my balls click to the on position and sperm started roiling around down there, and it was actually starting to shoot up my shaft. I was going to…I was going to…

"JOSHUA!"

Oh, fuck! I stuffed my rock hard cock, dripping and starting to drool, back into…into what? I was naked! And Misty was standing at the door, her arms folded across her beautiful chest, an angry look in her eyes.

"Josh," she strode into the room. "You know how I feel about you playing with yourself!" She actually leaned down and slapped my hand, which was on my dick, so it was like she was slapping me on the dick.

I cringed, at the pain and the humiliation.

She grabbed my ear and literally lifted me out of the chair. I took my hands away from my cock and it bounced up, red and ready to shoot.

"Look at you! Just like a bad, little boy! Can't keep your hands off yourself!"

"But…but…honey!"

"But nothing! You come back to bed this instant."

"But…but it was you? I was doing it to you! I found your channel! I was…it was like I was making love to you!"

"Oh! You are making me angrier and angrier! To think you are doing that filthy thing to…to me!"

"Wait a minute! Wait!"

I managed to loosen her grip on my ear and I stopped. She whirled around and face me, and her boobs went back and forth.

"What's the difference between me jacking off to you…and everybody on the internet jacking off to you?"

She had an answer, of course. "I don't know that anybody is masturbating to me. But I do know that you are masturbating, and it is a vile and evil thing sexual relations should be between a man and a woman not a man and his hand it's like you're cheating on me and…"

She went on and on. There was no end to her anger.

I finally managed to insert, "But I wanted to make love to you... but...you wouldn't..."

"I wouldn't because you are too slow. You're not a premature ejaculator...you're a postponed ejaculator! Maybe if you'd spend a little more time appreciating your wife then maybe..."and she was off again.

Feeling hang dog, I stood there and listened, and, finally, when she ran down, she grabbed my dick and pulled.

"Now get in that bed and don't move until you wake up!"

She pulled me into bed then climbed in after me. She spooned me, put her arms around me, one hand still gripping my aching, throbbing cock.

"Now I'm not going to let go until you wake up. So go to sleep."

I lay there, feeling her large breasts pressing against me, her hand holding my cock. And I was supposed to sleep? Hell! A dead man couldn't sleep if she was wrapped up against him like this. And I certainly wasn't dead!

Morning, and I yawned and felt like crap. I needed more hours of sleep. And I needed to get off. My dick was still hard. And her hand, though not closed, was resting on it.

Her hand. I was close. Maybe...maybe...I tilted my hips slightly.

Oh, fuck! Her hand closed! And it felt so fucking good! It felt like a vagina! I tilted my hips again and again, slowly pushing my cock into the circlet of her fingers, felt the warm flesh of her palm against my bulging veins.

"Good morning."

I froze.

She yawned and stretched, then hugged me again, and her hand ran into my iron cock. She giggled.

"Oh, that's nice. You wake up like this and I know you love me."

She began to stroke me, and pinch my nipples, and I groaned. I was going to get off...I was close...almost...almost...and...

RING RING!

The phone! At this time of the morning! Who the fuck...

The only thing Misty loves better than shopping is talking on the phone. She leaped over me and grabbed for her cell.

"Hello?" Was it my imagination? Or was she trying to sound a little...whispery? A little sexy, drawing her vowels out and...

"Oh, sure. I'll be there in a half hour. Bye!" She put her phone down.

"What?"

"That was the company. They need me for a photo shoot."

"This early in the morning?"

"Apparently my channel is taking off and they want to do some publicity photos. Isn't that great?"

"Uh…can we, uh…finish?"

"Oh, honey! I'm sorry, but I've got to go! I don't want to be late for fame and fortune, right?"

And, a few minutes later, as she went out the door, "You can watch my channel today, but remember…no yankie yankie!"

Oh, crap in a toaster. I NEEDED to whack off!

I went to work, and it hurt all day long, and I kept trying to focus on work, but it was hard! Hard working. Because of my hard. You get it.

But it was Friday, so I took off a little early and went home to watch Misty's channel.

I sat down and powered up the computer and tuned into the youtube channel. Misty's channel. And there she was.

Oh, fuck.

She was so beautiful, and her tits were so big, and I couldn't take my eyes off her lips, her red lips, whispering into the camera.

"Fuuuuck….IIII neeeeed yooooouuu! Myyyyy tiiits arrrre hoooot!"

They did a close up of her lips and I leaned up tot he screen. I stared at those lips that i knew so well. I stared at the redness, of the plumpness. I imagined kissing them, licking them, plastering my own lips against them. My dick was like a rod in my pants and I unconsciously divested myself of them. I sat there, naked from the waist down and lusted after my wife. I needed her. I wanted her. My ball sack felt full and tight. My balls were full of unexpended semen, and I needed to expend.

I found myself stroking. Stroking. God, she was beautiful. I wanted to hold her, feel those beautiful breasts. I wanted to…and I was getting close…my cock was rigid, hard, little bits of pre-cum flicked off the tip. I was almost there. I licked my own lips and gasped for breath and I was almost…almost…

"JOSHUA!"

Fuck! I jerked back and let go, and one, single drop of semen came to the slit and hung there.

She was home, Misty was home, and I almost sobbed.

She grabbed the back of my swivel chair and turned me around. My culprit dick stuck out, and she gasped and pointed at it. "What do you call that?"

I looked down at the single drop of sperm hanging, elongating, ready to drop. "A start?" My voice was choked up.

"You bad boy!" She slapped my dick. I yelped and it bounced up and down and the little drop of semen flew off. It didn't fly downwards, though, it flew upwards, and back, and hit me right in the mouth.

"Gah!" I blurted.

Misty stepped back in shock. "And you're eating it! You're eating your own...your own..."

"No!" I was starting to panic and I wiped my mouth off. "It just flew up and hit me! I don't do that!"

She took another step back, was outside the room. Her eyes were wide. "You really are a pervert."

"Honey! I'm not!"

But she turned and fled down the hallway. I followed her, and was just close enough to hear the bedroom lock click.

"Misty?" I tapped on the door.

"Go away!" I heard her crying. "Just go away and...and jack off!"

Fuck. Now I couldn't jack off. I was in trouble for jacking off. No way I was going to get in more trouble.

I finally left the bedroom door. I got out some blankets and prepared for a long night on the couch. At least she wouldn't be pressing her glorious body against me. (Sob!)

I settled in to watch some TV. I wanted to watch Misty's channel, I was feeling really horny after that, but I was afraid to. I was afraid I'd lose control and masturbate.

It was about nine o'clock when I finally heard the bedroom door open. I sat up and watched the hallway, and she came out of the hallway and entered the room.

She was naked—oh God!—and she came around the couch, grabbed the clicker and turned the TV off and sat down on the other side of the coffee table. Her eyes looked red, and her mascara had run. I had made her cry.

"Honey," I began. "I am—"

She held up a hand to stop me.

I stopped, but it was difficult looking at her in the eyes. She was naked. I think I mentioned that. But I was getting frazzled and unable to think.

"Joshua, we've got a problem."

"Yes, I know. I—"

"Please let me finish speaking."

I closed my mouth and listened. Sometimes this was good. She would talk for a while, get over her upset, and then we would have wonderful make up sex.

I wasn't prepared for what she was about to tell me, however.

"Joshua. You are a masturbator. And...I saw you with semen on your lips."

I started to protest but she held up her hand again. Which made her boobs bounce, and that certainly shut me up.

"Obviously I can't be married to a masturbator. I've got standards. I'm a public figure with a large following. I've got murals."

I started to tell her the word was morals, but stopped myself in time.

"I talked to the company, to my bosses, and they offered me a solution. I think the solution will work."

"Of course. Sure."

She frowned, I shut, and she continued.

"First, we need to do something about your penis. It is entirely out of control. All you want to do is play with it. That has to stop…"

"Of course. I promise—"

"…with a chastity belt."

My jaw dropped. My eyes blinked. My heart went 'what the fuck?'

"With a chastity belt we can stop you from abusing yourself, and you will be able to watch all the programming of me you want. In fact, my bosses have said you should watch all my programming. It is the best way for you to get over your preversions," I didn't correct her, "and they've even agreed to do special programming just for you."

"What?"

"They are preparing scripts for me to read that will address your problems specifically.

"Isn't that wonderful, Joshua? Isn't that kind of them? They will create programming that will specifically help people who have the jacking off problem, starting with you!"

"I…I don't know what to say."

"You don't have to know what to say. You simply agree, or we will not stay married."

I think, at that point, my mind broke into a thousand pieces, and the thousand pieces all got lost in some terrible hurricanic wind.

I loved my wife.

I was horny.

I needed my wife.

I was horny.

If I wanted my wife I had to wear this…this chastity thing.

But I was horny.

So, what can I say, I had no choice but to agree.

PART TWO

I was able to spend the night in the bedroom, which was a mixed blessing. On one hand I was forgiven, sort of, but on the other hand she had her arm around me and held my weenie.

I don't think I slept at all.

But Misty slept wonderfully. She even made sucking sounds, like she was chomping on my dick.

She awoke at 6 in the morning. Fresh and rested and ready for her youtube show.

I had big bags under my eyes.

She got up and fixed a big breakfast. Of mush and orange juice. Gah.

I had a couple of spoons of the glop, then got ready for work. Tying my shoes I was thinking about stopping off for a bag of donuts on the way to work, when…

DING DONG!

6:30 in the AM? Who the fuck could that be.

I opened the door, one shoe off and one shoe on. My fly down. "Yeah?"

"Special overnight delivery. Sign here."

Blinking, hardly awake, my eyes not awake enough to even read the return address, I signed, then brought the small box into the house.

"Who is it, hon?"

"I don't know?" I started opening the box and Misty entered the room.

Inside the box was another box, and inside that box was a black, velvet bag. And inside the black velvet bag were…I poured the contents out on the coffee table.

A banana shaped piece of plastic, several rings. A lock. "What the hell—"

"It's your chastity belt!"

"That's not a belt."

"It's a tube. Wasn't that nice of my bosses to overnight us a chastity tube?"

"I…" I thought they were king-sized assholes, but what could I say? "I think…yeah. It was nice of them."

"Take your pants down."

I did, and my boner was right there, saluting Misty like a private salutes a general.

43

"So much for that," I tried to hide my glee.

Misty frowned, then went into the kitchen. She came back with two bags of frozen peas. She placed the bags on each side of my penis and held them there.

"Ow! What the fuck!"

"Language, Joshua. Now take these and hold them. I'm not going to work until you have the chastity tube on. And you don't want to make me late."

I sat there, almost crying, as the peas froze my pecker. Slowly my boner shrunk, then shriveled, and shortly I had one of those little dingers that you get after swimming in cold water all day. Shriveled like a raisin.

"Excellent," crowed Misty. She picked up the tube and fit it over my cock. It slid on easy, lots of room. Then she put a ring around my package. A couple of tries and she had the right size. Meanwhile, my cock was starting to grow.

She fit the ring and the tube together, inserted the lock and snapped it shut, and, voila, I was rendered incapable.

In capable of fucking. In capable of jacking off. And, truth be known, incapable of even getting a hard on.

"Oh, fuck," I whimpered, as my cock filled the tube. Soon it was pressing almost painfully against the sides of the thing.

"Ooh, look how it's trying to squeeze through the little air slits. It looks all angry."

"Wouldn't you be angry if somebody tried to stuff you in a cigar box?"

She giggled. "You silly, that doesn't look anything like a cigar box. Besides, that tube is smaller than a cigar box."

"You're telling me," I scrunched over and held myself and willed the pain to go away.

"Now then, you go to work, and make sure you come home early enough to watch my show. Remember, it is aimed at preverts who masturbate too much.

"I can't jack off at all in this," I whimpered.

She smiled. "That's the point. Now, I'll see you tonight, don't wait up I might be late, and make sure you don't abuse your little peeny."

She walked out the door and I was left all alone. To whimper and cry. To feel my cock trying to grow big, getting hornier for trying to grow big, and then trying even harder to grow big.

Sadly, I went to work.

Work was half disaster, and half…something else.

The something else was that I threw myself into my work, tried to force myself to forget about my ever struggling cock.

The not something else, was that mid morning Bill Saunders came up to me and glanced down and whispered. "Looks like you're springing a leak."

I looked down at my pants. Sure enough, I was leaking. I was so horny the pre-cum was oozing out and soaking through my pants.

Now came one of the most embarrassing moments of my life.

I snuck into the ladies' room and stole a tampon. I wanted a kotex, but they only had a stack of free tampons.

I then went into the mens' room, and into a stall, and pulled the tampon apart, and stuffed it into my underpants.

It worked, the spread out tampon soaked up my juices, but...it felt weird.

Needless to say I spent the rest of the day hunkered down at my desk, my pants out of sight, and focused on work. And there's the good side again, I got a LOT of work done.

I was leaving when Chuck Evers called me into his office.

I sat down, put one leg over the other, realized that showed a bit of a wet spot, so I sat straight and took off my jacket and put it on my lap.

Chuck watched me for a moment, seemed a little confused by my goings on.

"What you need, Chuck?"

He focused on me, took the puzzlement off his face. "Oh, I just wanted to compliment you on your production, you're working really hard, but I noticed you're taking off a bit early. Any problems at home?"

Problems? Oh, fuck yes there were problems. My wife is on a sex channel and I'm wearing a chastity tube and I haven't had a cum in... in...I didn't know how long.

"No...no. I just..." I dwindled out.

"You're sure, because if there's anything we can do..."

"Well, I am sort of scrunched about something, would it be possible for me to do some of my work from home?" I had to get out of here. I felt like my pants were probably soaked through by now.

"Well, sure. We can try that. Company actually has a whole program designed for that. The Covid thing, you know."

"Oh, great."

"Tell you what, you have a good week end, relax, and I'll give you a call Sunday night and let you know."

"Oh, that would be great," my relief was evident.

"Excellent. Anything else we can do?"

"I think that's it, it sure would be a big help. Thanks."

"No guarantees yet, but..." he shrugged with a grin.

I got out of the car and looked down at the car seat. It was wet. I had actually dripped so much that I was leaving damp spots wherever I sat. NowI knew how women felt when they had their periods.

I walked into the house, changed clothes, and looked down at my prisoner. Mr. Happy squirmed within its cage. He was sort of multi-colored. Purple for the most part, but white where he was trying to sneak out the little openings on the sides of the cage.

And my balls hurt. Not bad, sort of like they had been kicked, but only by a midget. I could walk straight up, but I felt like I wanted to bend over and hold my balls all the time.

I went into the computer room and called up Misty's program, and my eyes bulged.

Yesterday she had had a few thousand followers for her channel. Now she had…A FEW HUNDRED THOUSAND!

Fuck! The world was tuning in to see my wife's body, to see her whisper obscenities and show off her boobs. But what could I do? I tuned in the program itself.

There was my wife, and she was in a new realm of excitement. She was talking into the camera, but her eyes gleamed with…with sexuality, almost like she was going to orgasm.

And her lips, so many close ups of them opening and closing, and looking like they were sucking on a dick, just from the simple act of talking.

And her tits were actually pink! They were glowing.

I watched, helplessly enraptured, as she said, "Fuuuck myyyy juuuuuicy hooooole. Eeeeeat meeee oooout! Stiiiick yoooour tooonguuue iiiintoooo meeee."

Suddenly I felt like the hairs at the back of my head were standing up. It felt weird, but powerful, and…and good. It was a nice sensation, and I felt my dick trying to erect even harder.

Oh, shit! This was supposed to be a program about not masturbating? It was making it harder and harder and…and if I didn't have the stupid cock cage on I knew I would be pounding my pud frantically.

I watched her beautiful lips kiss more words at me.

"Jaaaack ooooff. Preeeeteeeend yoooour haaand iiiis myyy puuuusssyyy! Preeeeteeeend IIIII aaaaaam suuuuuckiiiiing yoooou.

The feeling at the base of my scalp grew worse. I felt a delightful shiver shoot up into my skull, making my head feel light and airy and filled with glowy good feelings.

"IIIII waaaant tooo loooove yoooou wiiiith theeeese tiiitss." She cupped her breasts and held them up to the camera. "Suuuuck theeem. Leeeet meeee fuuuuck yooou wiiith theeem."

The feeling of shivers crept down my spine and I suddenly felt like my back was expanding.

I found myself sitting, helpless, and I felt a big splotch of water splatter on my caged cock.

I looked down, I was drooling. I was actually slack jawed, I had lost control of myself, and I was drooling like a baby that didn't know what its mouth was for.

Misty's lips moved, her breasts were on fire, her words went into my ears and caused a great soothing to enter my brain.

DON'T JACK OFF! The words appeared inside my cranium, flashed there as if made of neon. I should masturbate. I shouldn't…and my cock was so hard, struggling to be heard…and I had the feeling that my cock was screaming out that it didn't want to be masturbated.

What? But my cock always wanted to be masturbated!

"No, I don't," a voice said.

I blinked and looked up. I was no longer sitting in front of my computer. I was in a small, grey room. It looked like one of those interrogation rooms you see on cop shows. I was sitting at a table, my hands inside big chastity tubes, and the tubes fastened together by a length of chain at the tips. The chain went under a ring in the center of the table. I shook my arms, but the chain just rattled.

"Don't bother," somebody was speaking to me. I squinted my eyes. Who. was…who was…and I saw, on the far side of the table, sitting in a chair, my cock.

I know it was my penis. I recognized the shape of it. Hell, I had stroked it so often that I should recognize it.

"What…who…"

"I am your penis, Joshua…" the skull bent towards me and the slit turned into a mouth. A mouth with red, red lipstick. Lipstick the color of Misty's. And the lips looked like Misty's. It had two eyes, and the eyes looked like Misty's. "You've been a bad boy, Joshua. You've been abusing yourself. You've been abusing me."

"What? No! I…you…"

I was looking around frantically. this had to be a dream, a nightmare!

"Don't struggle Joshua, or I will make you cum."

The big penis sitting opposite me had a hand, and in the hand was a remote. The finger pressed the remote and I shivered and had an orgasm.

"Oh…oh…!" I looked down, semen was oozing out of the end of my cock cage. Just drooling out, never ending. "What is happening?" I sobbed.

"You've been bad, Joshua, and if you don't stop cuming I will go away. Your penis will go away, and there will be nothing left down there."

"This is crazy…this is insane…I can't…"

My dick pressed the button on the remote again.

I felt a fresh batch of goo slither out of the end of my cock. I looked down. It was a massive amount, and it ran down my legs and pooled on the floor.

"Stop cumming, Joshua. Stop being bad."

I was sobbing, and my hips were jerking, and the semen wouldn't stop pouring from my dick.

"If you don't stop I will go away. No more me. You will be left with nothing."

Again with the button, and more and more semen emitted from my caged cock. The floor was awash with my spunk. The floor was a shiny pool of white sperm.

"Stop, Joshua…stop…"

I kept crying, and she kept pressing the button…

"Joshua." My shoulder was shaking. "Joshua, wake up."

My eyes opened and I stared around wildly. The computer was off. No more Misty whispering her kisses at me. Telling me to stop masturbating…telling me I was going to lose my penis.

I turned, and there she was. In the flesh. I sobbed and grabbed for her. I put my arms around her waist and sobbed like a little baby.

"There, there…" she stroked my hair and held my face against her boobs. "You've been bad, but it's over. It's over now, Joshua."

I couldn't stop crying, and I held her. She let me, for a while, then she pried my arms loose. "Hush now, Joshua. Go fix dinner."

She left the room and I quickly followed her, my arms out, wanting her touch to reassure me. Oddly, my cock didn't hurt. I didn't even look down at it. But I was aware, in a vague, back of the mind way, that it wasn't struggling anymore.

She turned around and face me. She pointed towards the kitchen. "Dinner. Now. Then you must clean the dishes and do the laundry. This house is a mess, and you can make up for being bad by cleaning it. Now, go."

Refused her touch, I found myself following her orders. I went into the kitchen and began fixing dinner. I chopped vegetables and mashed potatoes. I put on a couple of lamb chops.

As I worked I looked at myself in the reflection in the window.

My hair was long, longer than it had been, and it hung half way down my face. I brushed it out of the way and continued preparing dinner.

And my face was softer. And my eyes were somehow doe-like, innocent.

I blinked, and perceived my body…my body…I lifted my tee shirt. I had little mounds on my chest, over the pectorals. And my nipples, they were bigger, and they were erect.

What was happening? But I automatically knew what was happening to me.

That dream...my penis talking to me...it...it was doing something to me. Something physical.

"Joshua, you have to control yourself."

Misty was standing int he doorway. She had showered and changed into a sexy dress. Funny, I wanted to see her naked, like on her youtube channel, but...but...

"Can you take off your clothes?"

"No, you silly." Then the strangest thing happened, she was standing there, arms folded, watching me, but it was like there was another one of her, bigger, behind her, over imposing on reality. And this bigger one said, "If you don't stop having those bad thoughts your penis is going to fall off."

I shook my head and the other Misty disappeared.

"What is it, Joshua."

"I...I..."

"You can talk. Tell me what is wrong."

"I saw two of you...and the other one told me my penis was going to fall off."

"Well, it will, silly Joshua, if you don't stop having those silly thoughts."

"What silly thoughts..." I was so confused...nothing made sense.

"Finish preparing dinner and I'll tell you. I'll be waiting to be served in the dining room."

I blinked, the dining room. I had to prepare a setting for her.

While the food cooked I took plate and cutlery out to the dining area. I poured a glass of water with a lemon wedge on the lip and took it out to her.

"Thank you, Joshua." She looked so gorgeous sitting there, at the head of the table, rolling her red, red lipstick on to her most perfect and plump lips.

I served dinner, and stood by the side and waited to make sure everything was perfect.

"This is delicious, Joshua. Thank you."

I glowed inside. I had never felt so happy.

She ate, finished, sighed and pushed her chair back. "Sit down, Joshua, it's time we had a talk."

Grateful, and feeling so proud to be allowed to sit in her presence, I took the chair she had indicated.

She sighed again, and watched me. "Joshua, Joshua, Joshua." Each word was like a benediction, and made me want to please her more and more.

"I should tell you about my new company."

I adored her.

"ASMR is designed to change men. These are implant programs, but they work on a physical level. You will have noticed that you are physically changing. And there are other programs which are designed to change women. That first day they had me watch a program, and I started waking up.

"I had been living a life to please men. The clothes I wore, the way I acted, it was all for men. I fixed you dinner and did the laundry, and it was all for you. Nothing for me.

"And while I slept in servitude the world went to hell. In a hand basket. Literally."

God, did I love her.

"So I watched a special ASMR for women and I awoke to who I was, what my true potential was. I was no longer the air-headed, big-titted bimbo living just to wait on my shallow husband, to suck his cock and lay down so he could cum in my pussy.

"And I found that I was not just a woman, but a special woman. I had talents which could be utilized to help change the world, to rid it of male enslavement, to right civilization, to resurrect a women ruled world, as it should be.

"The good news, I know that, you are happy to find yourself part of this new world order. You are loving the certainty of knowing your place.

"You like to serve women, you like it so much that you are becoming a woman. It's all in the ASMR implantation. You will change. You will grow large breasts and begin to color your lips. Your penis will disappear and you will live to serve me. You will make my life easier as I make the lives of the men and women of the world easier."

I wished she would let me slide out of this chair, crawl to her and suck her beautiful, red toes.

"Now then, Joshua...there will be many changes in the coming days, but all you have to do is keep watching the ASMR. Receive my message, and you will be happy. Is that understood?"

I wanted to kiss her red toes, and stroke my dick until I squirted all over them.

"Is that understood?"

Oh, with a shock I realized I was supposed to respond.

"Yes."

"Yes, ma'am."

"Yes, ma'am."

She smiled, and I about swooned.

"Then you may cum."

She snapped her fingers and I fell on my side, right out of the chair and onto the floor, and cum started pouring out of my little penis. I didn't have an orgasm, but i did release a large amount of spunk.

I stared in surprise at my penis. It was now so little it didn't really fill the cage. And my breasts. They were small, but they hung sideways on my chest, and I knew they were growing. And I felt so happy.

I looked up and Misty was still smiling down on me. She patted my long hair and said, "You won't need that chastity tube for long, but you will enjoy it. And it is necessary that you lose the ability to jerk off…the implantation program will work better if we control your juices."

I smiled, I loved the feeling of being deprived! But…but…"I'm cumming…but I'm not…there's no feeling…no orgasm."

She shook her head, "Joshua, Joshua. Don't you understand? Those days are over. You will have an orgasm, eventually, but not until we tell you to. You may go now."

I struggled to a kneeling position and started to stand up.

"Like that. Leave like that."

I knew what she meant. I might be allowed to walk upright later, but right now, in this moment of servitude being enforced, I was required to crawl. Like a dog. Like a pet. Like a person who, if they didn't serve well, might well end up in the back yard, in a doghouse, chained to a pole and allowed only to bark at intruders.

A MONTH LATER…

I scurried through the house checking myself.

My nails were done, long and red and quite perfectly polished.

My make up was done to perfection, and my long, lush hair was coiffed in the French style. Only a few wisps allowed to dangle about the ears.

I caught a glimpse of myself in the hall mirror.

My breasts were large and jutting, perfectly presented by my maid uniform. The maid uniform was tight about my waist, and the top was a thin, puffy blouse. My boobs jutted forth most deliciously.

The neatest thing, however, was my high heels. My heels were tall, my red toes peeking out the end, and my freshly shaved calves were curvy and woman powerful.

It had been such a hard month, not because I struggled against the changes, but because I tried to hard to keep up with the changes.

I was a woman now. My vagina had finished forming, my dick was no more, and I lived to serve.

"Josie!" Misty called.

"Yes, ma'am," I hurried down the hall, my high heels clicking on the wood floor that I had lavished so much attention on.

I had lavished attention on everything. The grass was cut so that all blades were a scant half inch. It looked more like a carpet than a lawn out there.

The floors were washed and polished to a glossy shine.

The windows were sparkling clean. The drapes had been brushed, the furniture polished, and…and everything was perfect.

"Yes, ma'am," I stepped into the living room and stood at attention.

"Is everything prepared?"

"Yes, ma'am. The kitchen has been cleaned. The shrubs have been trimmed, the…" I ticked off items on my fingers.

Misty listened, and I marveled at how she had changed.

She was a bit taller now, actually taller than me, and I knew this trend would continue. Her hair positively glowed with health. Her eyes possessed a sparkle that warmed the world. Certainly warmed me.

And her body, already amazing, was even more amazing. Her skin was glowing, her muscles had shifted and she was totally statuesque. Really an amazing example of womanhood.

And there was not even the slightest hint of the air-head she had once been. Not in looks, nor in speech, nor in action.

"Excellent," she said, when I was finished with recounting the tasks I had completed. "Remember, best behavior. My visitors are very important, and I wish to make a good impression."

"Yes, ma'am."

KNOCK KNOCK.

She motioned with her head and I ran for the door. Through the living room window I caught a glimpse of the large, black truck parked in front of the house. A bevy of security vehicles surrounded it. Out of the security vehicles poured a veritable army of women.

Tall women in strict uniforms. Tall women with large breasts, long hair tied back, body armor that couldn't conceal their robust charms.

I opened the door and four of the women entered. Glanced at me, and one frisked me, which gave me quite a thrill, then they spread out through the house, and more women entered.

I stood to one side and watched the women sitting in the garden. We had a large backyard, and a suitable house, so we had been chosen for this meeting.

Among the women sitting was my wife, looking so incredibly beautiful Surrounding her were more women like her. Leaders of industry, celebrities, all stunningly beautiful.

At points around the yard the ladies of the security detail held their posts, watching over everything.

Suddenly there was a stir, a few heads turned, and excitement ratcheted up.

"She's coming!"

"She's here!"

Oddly, I didn't know who was coming. Just that she was a very important person. I had been working too hard to even think about who our illustrious visitor would be.

Four security guards entered through the side yard, took places, and then she walked into the backyard.

She was eight feet tall. Maybe taller, and a more gorgeous specimen of womanhood I had never seen.

She must have weighed 400 pounds, but she was perfectly formed. A 6 foot woman might be 36 by 24 by 36. She was at least 48 by 36 by 48.

Her face was large, her lips huge, but merely perfectly shaped and appropriate for her size.

Her hair was long, golden, almost glowing with health and goodness.

Most amazing of all, however, was her presence, her ambience. She exuded a glow that touched all, elevated all. Just to be around her was to feel her uniqueness, her goodness.

I found that my legs were trembling and my hands were shaking. I felt her goodness reach out and touch my heart. I would have collapsed, except...she wouldn't let me. Her presence required that I stay and remain aware. Fully aware. More aware than I had ever been.

There were a few handclaps, soft things, but more mutterings, soft whispers of appreciation.

The giant woman walked past the gathered women and stood in front of them. She needed no dais as she was head and shoulders taller than all.

She smiled, and I felt, as no doubt every woman in the backyard felt, that the smile was directed solely at me.

"Good afternoon," her voice was a pleasing symphony of nuances and bells.

"I am Silithia, and I welcome you all to our new world.

"You have already experienced the world that is coming, and our progress will be magnificent in the coming months.

"Men are being transformed, and worthy men, the true Alphas, are being herded for service."

There was a quick murmur, and Silithia smiled.

"I know, it is so discouraging to have to make love to a beta man, but we will shortly have large dicked men at your service.

"Now then, the purpose of this meeting is to acquaint you with certain factors that will aid in the transition of the world. ASMR is only one of our magnificent programs, and...

She went on and on, and her words were a blessing. She explained about herself, and how we should respond to the coming changes. I began to understand that I wasn't just a beta, but was even above an Alpha. I was being allowed to transform into the highest form of life...a woman.

A world where everybody knew their place, and were content with it.

Beta men to serve in the fields and factories. Alpha men to provide the real needs of love and sexuality. And people like me, allowed to ascend to womanhood.

Eventually I would be a real woman, and I might even be allowed access to the path that Silithia was laying out, to become a giantess, like her.

It was an amazing future, and I couldn't wait for it. I couldn't... Silithia stopped talking. The meeting was over and she was taking the time to do a meet and greet.

I moved to accommodate the flow of the crowd, to serve drinks and treats.

Silithia didn't move much, at first. She was the center and the crowd crushed in on her. I was aware of her security forces taking a powerful stand, protecting her at all costs.

I kept returning to the kitchen for tray after tray of champagne. I stepped out of the kitchen at one point and froze.

Silithia was standing right in front of me, her back to me, and I started to back up...except I was frozen by her goodness.

She turned and smiled down on me. "And here we have a fine example of a New Woman." Everybody was silent as she touched me with her presence. "Tell me, dear, how do you like being a woman."

I began to cry, deep sobs of gratitude.

Silithia nodded. She reached out and touched me in the center of my chest with one finger.

"You have worked so hard, you deserve your first female orgasm."

A burst of white hot heat through my chest, expanding outward, flowing through my limbs. I didn't have a dick anymore, but I did have female plumbing, and it began to convulse. My pelvis shimmied and quaked, my knees gave way and I collapsed. I lay on the ground, a puddle of an earthquake of orgasm. I couldn't move, I could just gasp as the massive sensation had its way with me.

"And that is how we treat the New Woman," Silithia chuckled and stepped over me.

Other woman passed over me, around me, and I lay on the ground, helpless in the throes of the ultimate sexual experience. I hadn't just had an orgasm...I WAS an orgasm.

Time passed, and I slowly came to myself. Dazed, I sat up and leaned against the wall.

Silithia was gone, along with her security guards and all the women. The backyard was empty.

Misty was sitting in a nearby chair, watching me.

"Oh..." I said.

She grinned.

"How was it?"

"I never...I never..."

"Well good. You did a good job, and you should be rewarded. And now you know your true place in the New World Order."

"Yes, ma'am." I struggled to stand up.

Misty stood up and came to me, helped me stand on my own two feet. "Who knows," she mused. "They might even allot you time with one of the Alpha men."

Slowly, I stopped shaking.

"Would you like that?"

"Oh, yes ma'am."

"Good. And you may address me as Misty. You've changed, and while you are still in servitude, you have earned the right to address another woman by name."

"Yes, ma'am. Misty."

She patted my cheek, "Now clean up this mess."

She turned and walked away, and I stared at her form, her curves, her large breasts and round hips. And I could feel her goodness emanating, touching all reality with the unique wonderful essence that is the spirit of an enlightened and transformed woman.

I was lucky. Once I had been a man. A sniveling, creepy perversion of masturbation and self satisfaction. Now I had a chance to be a woman, a real woman, and all that that entailed.

The world would now be a better place.

I turned to the backyard and began cleaning up.

END

AUTHOR'S NOTE

You can read about Silithia, where she came from, how her beliefs were formed, and how she intends to change the world, in the book of her name.

SILITHIA

You may also read of her adventures in

WOMANLAND

and various stories available at

GROPPER PRESS

Thanks for reading and…HAVE A HORNY DAY!

Grace Mansfield

Full Length Books from Gropper Press

Rick Boston and his beautiful wife, Jamey, move to Stepforth Valley, where Rick is offered a job at a high tech cosmetics company. The House of Chimera is planning on releasing a male cosmetics line, and Rick is their first test subject. Now Rick is changing. The House of Chimera has a deep, dark secret, and Rick is just one more step on the path to world domination!

The Stepforth Husband

Super Rabbit Sex Pills

An adventure in over sexualization!

PART ONE

"Oh! Oh!" Jackson thrust his hips a final time, and I felt the splattering of semen in my vaginal canal come to an end.

"Oh, wow!" He rolled off me and laid on his back, staring at the ceiling.

And I felt...empty.

"Hey," I said.

"That was good, wasn't it?" he whispered to me. He was already starting to drift off.

I rolled on my side and shoved him.

"What?" He blinked, and I could tell that he was irritated. Man cum. Man go sleep. Grrr.

"I didn't cum!"

"So...go ahead and cum." He closed his eyes and tried to drift off again.

I shook him. "With your dick. Hello...I need your stiff rod."

He smiled dreamily. "So sorry, rigid was a few minutes ago. Time for noodle to take over."

"Noodle isn't worth a damn!"

He was trying to ignore me. "I know...but I'm...tired."

He snored.

I lay back on my back and sighed in frustration. Man cums, has his big orgasm, and the hell with women. And it seems that was always the way it was. At least that's the way it had been for every man I had been with.

Damn!

So I reached my fingers down and started to scratch my itch. And got a big, slippery hunk of goo for my troubles.

Crap! I wiped my fingers on the bed spread. Just once...just once I would like to be the one that came, and left him all gooey. Let him clean up his mess, sleep in the wet spot. I'd like to see how happy he was then!

His snores picked up in volume. I pulled a pillow over my head and held it tight. I could still hear the snores.

I rolled over, turned away from him.

Maybe if men could experience what it was like to be left all frustrated, then they wouldn't be so willing to turn over and snore. Maybe then they'd show a little consideration and…and…something was nibbling at my consciousness. Something about men cumming, and ejaculating. They squirted fast and they rolled over. But what if women squirted and rolled over. How would they like that?

And. I started thinking about it.

Men. Women. The difference between. And that little piece of something that had been nibbling at my awareness finally came into view.

Men cum. Lots of sperm.

But women actually cum, too. Just not as much. So what if I could shift the balance? What if I could make it so it was the other way around?

Hmmm.

Suddenly I wasn't dozing. I was thinking.

It didn't take much for me to get my bosses on board. Of course, there was good reason for them to want to be on board.

First, clinical studies get good government grants. Anything that smacked of women's rights and the government bent over and spread their legs.

Second, my bosses are women. Sure, there was my official pitch, which they listened to politely. And they read my research paper on the possibilities, but the real clincher was when they talked to me outside official channels. They would run into me while I was going to my car, or riding the elevator, or even in the bathroom.

"What are the real ramifications for your project, just between you and me."

And I would say something like, "Don't you ever get tired of sleeping in the wet spot?" Which worked fine except for Martha Vanes. She was gay, no wet spot for her. But, being gay, she was on board anyway.

Go gay!

Anyway, I got my funding and began the heavy lifting.

First, ten tons of paper. Lots of letter writing, setting up physical trials, contacting various. agencies. But I had been to school, I knew about paper shuffling. I was good at paper shuffling.

Jackson was interested. I wasn't talking much, which created a mystery, but he knew large amounts of money was coming through my department, I was having weekly talks and meetings with the bigwigs, and he overheard bits and pieces from his perch in front of the TV.

"You're going to reverse what?"

I went glib, even to my man, who I trusted more than anybody. "It's more of a balancing act. Leveling the playing field between men and women."

He yawned, "Say what?"

"If we can increase the amount of fluid in the female bladder it will self-cleanse. This benefits men, as it will..." blather, blather, blather.

I watched him carefully to make sure he was properly lulled.

I loved Jackson, but he was eye candy, and boy toy, and booty call, and I was tired of him rolling over and leaving me high and dry.

"So if we can reduce the amount of prolactin and oxytocin in the male system, which will relieve stress, boost the immune system and protect against heart disease, then he will last longer in bed and..." which meant that he wouldn't be able to cum so easy, and would last longer and finally please me.

"Then the female ejaculate won't be re-absorbed and women will experience relief from headaches, menstrual cramps, back pain and..." which meant that women will cum faster, and they will put out more ejaculate...for his wet spot.

Snore. Jackson gave up trying to understand and slept right through two MMA matches on the TV.

It took a year. Eleven months of getting the funding and filling out the paperwork, then a month of actual experimentation.

Lord, we killed a lot bunnies, but it was all in the name of science, and it was obvious that it was all going to work...so a single year and we had a pill. Man, I couldn't wait to try it out.

Actually, we had had two pills, and, being cute, we made one pink and one blue.

And, since we had had such success with bunnies, I took a pair of pills home to Jackson.

I fixed him a big steak dinner. A ton of mashed potatoes on the side, and Moose Tracks ice cream for desert. Man, he was in hog heaven.

Then I fixed him a big drink. Then another one and another one.

Finally he was fat and happy.

"Man," he belched, "That was one good dinner! What's the occasion," he asked.

I smiled. "I'm glad you asked.

His eyes were wandering a little bit, so I knew I better keep the explanations to a minimum. I didn't want him sleeping before I got him to take the pill. That would sure be a colossal waste of Moose Tracks.

"I picked up some, uh, multi-vitamins this afternoon. We need to have a healthier lifestyle. You want to live to be old, right?"

"Oh, yeah," he yawned.

Fuck, too much Coke and bourbon.

"Here. Here's your vitamin." I handed him the blue pill.

He took it, looked at it, and yawned. "I don't know...I'm pretty healthy right now. Do I really need another vitamin? What if I get too healthy?"

Argh! Bone-headed males!

"Here, let me suck on your penis for a while."

He perked right up.

I extracted his slack weenie and got it hard. I began to slurp on it, and in between slurps I encouraged him.

"Come on, Jackson. Eat your vitamin. It'll be good for you."

"Uh...oh...yeah! That feels good."

"It'll feel better if you take your pill."

"Ummm....ooh. Fuck!"

I was deliberately going slow, drawing it out, hoping to put the pressure on him. But he didn't seem to be getting it. He bent down, he was going to lift me up, throw me down and fuck me.

Fuck!

So when he lifted, for a moment his mouth was open, and I popped the pill into his mouth.

He blinked as the pill hit the back of his throat. Then he convulsively gulped and the pill rolled right down his throat and splashed into his belly.

"Wha...what was..."

"Oh, shut up," and I kissed him. And kissed him, and totally distracted him from the pill episode.

He fell back on the couch and I crawled over him. Now that he had taken the pill, now that I had achieved my goal, I could admit to a certain degree of horniness. Though, to be honest, I wasn't sure if I was horny because I was horny, or because I had managed to get Jackson to take the pill, and was looking forward to a lifetime of no wet spots, his reduced ejaculation, and my increased ejaculation.

I mounted him and felt for his dick. Good, nice and hard, and the tip felt so good. I placed it between my labia and started to slide down his shaft.

Oh, God! It felt good! That big head opening me up, feeling the veins ripple along my vaginal walls, and when I bounced off those balls he grunted, and I almost came right there.

Except that Jackson spurted when I hit his balls. So he spurted, and I almost spurted, and once again I was left with a wet spot.

Son of a bitch!

But, it wasn't too bad. Since I was on top, when he fell out all the gism plopped down on him. He he!

Later, getting ready for bed, I thought of all the wonderful changes. He would be harder for longer, and he would be desperate to cum, and that would make him fuck harder. I would get orgasms, maybe even lots of orgasms, and I could, for once, leave him high and dry.

I sat on the toilet and peed and dreamed of all the great cums I would have, and I reached over for my pink pill. Jackson got blue and I got pink. I would squirt sooner and he would squirt later, finally a balance achieved.

I opened my pill box and took out my pill and—stop. Fuck. Oh, no! OH...FUCKING...NO!

I was holding the blue pill. That's right, Jackson had taken the pink one. He had taken the wrong pill. That stupid…

I jumped up, then sat down. I wasn't done peeing and the seat was splattered. Imagine that, me peeing on the seat.

As the last dribbles came out my mind was working furiously.

I swapped chemical formulas in my mind. I reversed formulas and applied them to opposing DNAs.

What if he began to squirt even faster? And what if I got even slower? That would be a disaster of biblical proportions.

But, wait a minute, most of the chemicals were the same, it was just a few things, and a variance in amounts, so it should work…but I couldn't take a chance.

I jumped up and ran into the bedroom.

Jackson was already snoring. Fuck!

I jumped on his belly and he oofed and sat up. "What the fuck?" he gasped.

"You've got to…you've got to…" I grabbed the back of his head and stuck my fingers down his throat.

"GAAA!" a huge glop of steak and Moose Tracks hurled at me. The ice cream was mixed with stomach fluids, and the steak came out in chunks, and I looked at myself in disgust. I was covered with the vile goop.

"What the fuck!" he sputtered as he spit out bits and pieces. "What are you doing?"

"Look at me!" My front was coated with his disgusting dinner, and the smell was terrible.

"Fuck. Look at me!" He was similarly covered with vomit. "What the fuck did you—"

"Quick, do you see the pill on me?" I began digging my fingers through the upchuck that covered us. It was like combing through skunk stew.

"What…what are you…"

"The pill! You took the wrong one! Do you see it on me?"

I was combing his front, and he finally figured it out and began combing his fingers through my front.

For a long minute we examined the puke. We put the bits of steak in one pile, no pill there. We scooped the soupy stuff off and examined that. No pill.

"Oh, fuck!" I whispered.

He looked at me, his face white, "What's going to happen to me?"

I blinked, then tried on a rueful grin. "Probably nothing." I mean, it's just a vitamin, right?"

"Then…then why did you stick your fist halfway down my throat?"

"I, uh…I love you?"

"Heysoos Xristo, Judith! Look at me! Look at this mess?"

"Well, I'm sorry, I just thought…I was a little worried…but…"

So I took the wrong pill and you reach down and pull the contents out of my stomach. And for what? I don't get it!"

He got out of bed, picked up the sheets and walked them through the house and into the garage. He returned, trying not to drip vomit on the floor, and went into the shower.

I stood there and thought about what I had done.

So what if I had given him a rather strong female pill. It wasn't like he would turn into a woman or anything, right?

The most that would happen is that his sexual activities might jump, or wane, or something, for a while. Right?"

By the time he got out of the shower I had convinced myself that everything was all right, and I even smiled at him as I went to get into the shower.

And, as I soaped myself and rinsed all of his accident off me I was pretty sure that there would be no bad effects. Everything was going to be all right.

Which is not to say that I didn't look into the effects of the male sex taking the wrong pill.

I quickly lined up a few rabbit cages in a corner of the lab and selected a half a dozen male rabbits. Then I injected them with the essence of the pink pills.

Nothing happened.

But I held off on taking my own pill. After all, I wanted to be sure, and better to be safe than sorry.

The day passed, and I kept checking on the rabbits. They humped each other, but that was normal for bunnies. They hump anything and everything. So no alarm there.

By end of day I was convinced that it had all been a false alarm. No change to the bunnies, so there would be no change to Jackson.

I sighed with relief as I turned off the lights and went home.

I kept a low profile for the next few days. Jackson was pretty pissed off about how I'd fisted his throat, and he grumped mightily about having to wash his vomit covered sheets. Well, I wasn't going to wash them! It had been his vomit, after all.

But, men get angry, then they get horny, then they get over angry. By that weekend he was feeling randy, so I would let him make love to me, and I didn't even think about him leaving me a wet spot. I was too busy thinking about how to get him to take the right pill.

"Honey," he said, rolling over and poking me in the backside with his maleness, "I think we should, uh…you know?"

Good. No anger, and maybe I could sneak a pill into him.

I roll over and grabbed his weenie, and my hand slipped right off it.

I looked down and it was small.

But he didn't notice. He was too horny to notice anything. I looked at him and covered up my surprise.

He was shrunken. Was this an effect of the pink pill? Was he going to notice? And, more important, was he going to get all upset and blame me?

Gosh I didn't want any male drama. I didn't want to hear him bitching and whining about how I made him take the pill. It's a free country, after all.

I kissed him, and managed to hold his teeny weenie, and I started thinking. If he had a teeny weenie, maybe he would have less sperm. It made sense, and there was only one way to find out.

He kissed me back, then went for my chest.

I have a healthy set of lungs and it felt good to have him fondle and suckle.

But I had to find out about that weenie.

He started to reach down for his dick and I stopped him. I didn't want him noticing how small he was.

"Let me," I said.

He lay on his back, a big grin on his face, and I mounted him. I sat astride him and held his dick firmly. Fortunately, it was hard. Harder, in fact. It was hard as a button.

Carefully, I sat down, slipped his weeny into me, and…it was less than thrilling. I've never been a size queen, but a girl's got to have some heft to her invader, right?

But he didn't notice. He just started pumping. Really fast.

REALLY fast.

A crazed look came into his eyes, then he flipped me over, keeping himself pressed hard against me, and he kept pumping.

I could hardly feel his member, it was like a finger, but he could feel it. His eyes went blank and he started drooling and his hips moved like they were jet propelled, little jerks, ten times a second, rapid, frantic, and I couldn't even move. I couldn't respond, he was too fast. He was to…

"Eeeh….Iiiiii….eeeewww!"

He began to squirt, huge gouts of male batter. I could feel him filling my hole, then the stuff was overflowing, getting all over everything, and still he made squeaking sounds and kept spewing that obnoxious stuff out.

I pushed him off and rolled away, I slipped off the bed and stared at him.

"EEEEEEE! IIIIII!" Such a high voice, and that tiny weeny was squirting and squirting, I had never seen so much cum in my life! It was like that tiny weeny was a full sized garden hose. The bed was a mess, goo was dripping off the mattress and onto the floor, and he was still jerking his hips. Then he was slowing down, his spasmodic hips slowed down, and the sperm came to a trickle, then it ended.

He was unconscious. Laying there in a puddle of his own squirtem.

"Jackson!" I shrieked.

I went to him, almost slipped in the mess pooling around the bed, and felt his pulse. It was there, in fact it was hard and fast. Really fast, but he was…he was…SLEEPING!

He had squirted a stupendous load then simply fallen asleep! So fast…and I won't even talk about the fact that I felt nothing. I was so less than satisfied…oh my God!

"Jackson! Wake up!" I shook him hard.

Slowly, his eyes opened. He looked dazed and...and happy! Supremely happy. Sublimely happy.

"Oh, man, that was good. Was it good for you?"

"You son of a bitch!" I cried. I pulled him off the bed, and now we both slipped in the goo and fell on our asses.

Still, he was not completely aware. He was just confused, and he had this dopey look on his face.

"What's the matter. What's..."

I pushed him towards the shower. A minute later he was singing lustily in the shower, happy as a clam that hasn't been shelled.

I looked at the mess he had made of my bedroom. Cum covering the bed, dripping off the sides like icing off a cake. The floor was a huge puddle around the bed. And there were splatters on the ceiling and the wall next to the bed.

Holy fuck! I thought. And I realized, *The pink pill!*

The pink pill had gone into effect. It had made him squirt more, like it was supposed to make a woman have more ejaculate. but the amount of time...and I figured it out. His hips had been moving so fast, faster than one of the rabbits in my experiment. How many hip thrusts does a man have during sex...a hundred? But he must have had a thousand thrusts, just at a high rate of speed, so it had taken him longer to cum. His body had adapted, but...it must have adapted to more speed so he would time to cum before the woman gave out.

At that I was sore down there. The front of my body hurt where he had slammed into it, and I had managed to escape halfway through.

Fuck!

The shower door slammed, he came into the room rubbing his body with a towel. I got a good look at his penis. It had been 7 inches. Now it was about three, and it was still hard!

He looked at the bed and his mouth opened and shut. "Holy fuck! What happened?"

"You happened!" I said, suddenly weary.

He looked at me then. I was covered in sperm. It was caked all over my front, on my face, in my hair, I was covered like I had been dipped in the stuff.

"Oh, my God! Are you all right?"

Angrily, I brushed past him and headed for the shower. Just as I was stepping into it he screamed.

"EEEEEEEE!"

I ran back into the bedroom, he had finally noticed his penis.

"What the fuck!" His voice was high pitched and frantic. "What happened to my dick."

"It's okay…it's all right!"

"Fuck you say! Somebody stole my dick! It's never going to be all right!"

"Well, he kept yelling and carrying on, I finally stepped up and slapped him in the face.

He blinked and held his cheek and stared at me, then he started crying. He sobbed and sobbed, and cried and cried. He cried just like… like a little girl.

That Saturday was a mess.

First he cried about his weenie, then he cried that I hit him, and it was like he was having hormones or something.

To make matters worse, he was worthless at cleaning up his mess. I mean it was his sperm, right? So he should have been the one to wash his sheets and clean the carpet.

But he was so busy wailing and howling that I had to put it in the wash, and I had to go rent a carpet cleaner.

Then, when I finally got everything cleaned up, he had the nerve to ask me for dinner.

Crap! I had worked all day, I was tired, and now he wanted me to fix dinner?

So I started to fix dinner, and he came in and stood behind me at the sink.

"What?" I asked, a little peeved at the way this day had gone.

"I…uh…."

He sounded contrite, and I sighed.

"I'm…uh…"

I reached for a towel, which meant I had to bend over a little more, and suddenly he was on me. I was trapped against the sink, his weight held me, and it was like he was trying to get his little weenie inside me., but he was wearing clothes.

He began humping me, his hips jerking back and forth at that frantic ten times a second pace.

Oh, fuck!

I tried to yell, but he was pummeling me and I couldn't g et a breath. I mean, it wasn't like I was getting raped, his weenie wasn't long enough for that, but I was pinned in place, and I could feel his weenie rubbing between my buns. Back and forth, frantic, desperate, moving like a hummingbird's wing.

"Sto…sto…stop!"

But he wasn't stopping. He was like a maniac!

I saw his face in the window reflection, his eyes were glazed and there was not a trace of intelligence. He was just an out of control fucking machine!

"Eeeh…eeeh…eeeh…eeeh…" he made that funny, high pitched sound, like he was moaning, but in fast time. Unbelievably fast time.

Finally, he started quirting. His hips locked for a split second, pumped, locked again, pumped.

I managed to push back and get him off me. I turned around and stared at him.

He was staggering back against the stove, his pants were turning wet and I could see little bulges in his crotch, again and again, and I knew he was spurting.

"Heysoos Xristo!" I blurted. "Are you crazy?"

He didn't hear me, he just slid down the front of the stove, his hips jerking and locking, jerking and locking, and the cum was seeping through his pants, getting all over the floor.

He began to slow down, just twitches, then he was done. He was laying on his side and snoring deeply.

I stared down at my mess of a hubby. Wtf! Wtf!

Snore. Snore. Deep gasps of sleep that showed how much he had exhausted himself.

That was the moment that I realized that I might have a wee bit of a problem.

"Okay, that should do you."

"But, honey?" He stared up at me.

He was laying on my freshly made bed. He was wearing a garbage bag around his midsection. I had cut holes and taped it on him and I figured that would keep his slime in his own pants.

"Do we have to do this?"

I had put handcuffs on him, and the handcuffs were looped over a chain, which chain was around one of the bedposts.

"We do this until you get a little self control. Have you looked at yourself lately?"

"But I can't help it! I don't know what's wrong! I just start to feel horny, and then everything blanks out until I wake up and find out that I've...I've..."

"You've made a mess, and I can't have any more of that."

He started to cry, and I started to think that the pink pill had loosed a torrent of hormones.

I lay down next to him, my back to him, I wasn't too happy with my cum crazy husband, and went to sleep.

Snore. Snore.

RING RING!

What the fu—? I came out of a deep sleep and looked around.

Jackson was still sleeping. the pillow was over his head so he hadn't heard the phone.

I slipped out of bed and lurched across the room. I picked up my phone and answered it in a soft voice as I left the room.

"Judith?"

I recognized the voice of my lab assistant.

"Yeah?"

"You need to get down here."

"What happened? What's going on."

"I can't tell you. You just need to get down here."

Man, she sounded disturbed. I hung up the phone and went back into the bedroom. Quickly, I pulled on clothes. Jackson heard me and stirred.

"Judith?" he mumbled.

"It's okay," I said. "I have to go to work."

"Can't we make love before you go?"

Crap. It had only been a few hours and he was ready to go again.

"No time now. Maybe when I get back," not.

"I need...I need..."

I stared down at my bone-head hubbie. He was awake now, and his hips were moving back and forth slowly. Shit. It wouldn't be long until they were moving back and forth frantically. Well, no help for it.

I leaned over and gave him a kiss, "Work emergency. I'll be back in an hour." I hoped.

"But...I need it. I need love. I've got to..."

"Just control yourself," I turned the light off and headed out the door.

I heard him calling for me, but I was in a hurry. I went out the door and was shortly speeding down the street. I was biting my lip and wondering what had happened. I had never received a call in the middle of the night before, it must be some hellacious emergency.

I wheeled my Miata into the parking lot and into my space. I grabbed my purse and hurried for the door. I slid my card through the reader, pushed through the door, and waved at the security guards who had suddenly woken up.

"It's just me..."

I don't know if they knew me, but I was in too much of a hurry to waste time by chatting with them.

Through the double doors, down the hall and through the main lab.

"I'm back here, Judith!"

I hurried through the lab to the bunny room. I stepped in and stopped.

In a far corner of the room six cages were open and the bunnies were lying on the floor. They were covered in white fluid and were dead, their eyes glazed and unseeing.

"What the hell happened?"

Sandy, my assistant was lifting the last rabbit down to the floor. As I approached I could see the rabbit's penis.

Normally a rabbit's penis is small and covered with fur. This one was smaller than normal, but the fur had been rubbed off, and the skin was rubbed off, too.

"They started…humping. But they didn't have anything to hump so they just humped their door latches. That's the only projection in the cage. They humped and I couldn't stop them.

That one there humped so hard he broke his door. He fell on the floor and kept jerking and twitching, then he just…died!

I took the bunny from her hands. Yes. The penis was half size, and the rabbit had rubbed through the skin. There was blood, but there was also semen, bunny semen, all over it.

"Did they…do they all have this amount of ejaculate?"

"Yes. And it's a lot. I measured bunny J, he didn't break out of his cage and the …the bunny sperm stayed mostly in the cage. There's a half a cup of sperm on the floor of his cage.

I looked into bunny Js, cage. He was gone, dead on the floor, but the cup Sandy had used to measure was still in there, slightly over half a cup of semen, We were using Eastern cottontails, and they weighed about 2.5 pounds. A half a cup weighed four ounces. Holy Heysoos in leaky galoshes! the bunny had ejaculated 10% of his total weight! That was… that was…impossible!

And it was no wonder the rabbits had died.

In a back portion of my mind I started doing calculations, translating bunnies to humans. Jackson weighed 160 pounds. He had cum an easy cup, probably more. But 16 ounces to 160 pounds, translate liquid measure to body weigh, carry the 10, multiply…my eyes opened.

"Jackson!" I yelped. "Oh, my God!"

Judith stared at me. "What?"

"Jackson! I gave him the…he's cumming too much…he's…oh, my God!" and I ran out the door.

PART TWO

I skidded to a stop in the driveway, nearly taking out the mail box on the way in. I ran into the house, slamming open the door.

"Jackson!" I yelled

From the back of the house I heard that weird rabbity orgasm sound. "Eeeee….ug….Eeeee!"

I sprinted down the hallway and into the bedroom.

Jack was on the bed, right where I had left him. He was stretched out, on his back and shooting cum. Gallons of cum. Cum on the ceiling, cum on the walls, and his little pecker was squirting up in the air like a geyser. He had broken through the black garbage bag and was really letting loose!

"Jackson!" I screamed. I leaped on the bed and looked down. He was out of it. He was making sounds, squirting like it was his last cum (and it might well be) and his eyes were open and vacant. He wasn't even aware of what he was doing.

I slapped him. I didn't know what else to do.

He didn't notice. Another mighty squirt of semen.

I punched him in the gut, and that made him twitch, but his groin erupted yet again.

So I did the only thing I could think of, I grabbed his package in my hand and twisted.

"OW!" And his eyes blinked.

I twisted so hard I was afraid I would twist them right off.

His eyes opened more, the semen squirt was less, and he started to look at me.

"Judith? Judith? Ow!"

I let go and got the key to the handcuffs off the side table and unlocked him.

"Oh, Jackson!" I hugged him.

"Why do my nuts hurt?" he asked.

"Because you came too much!" I cried.

"Oh. It was feeling good for a while. What happened? Why is this happening to me?"

"The pink pill you took last week."

"The pink...but I thought I threw it up?"

"Apparently you didn't"

He was hugging me back now, and coming to himself more and more.

"What can I do?"

Ah, that was the question now, wasn't it?

We sat at the kitchen table drinking Coke and bourbon. He needed fluids of any kind. He actually looked wan, like he had lost so much liquid that his cheeks were hollow.

I needed a drink because it is a well known fact that drinking helps your thinking.

"So it's the pink pill that's making me cum so much...and it shrank my dick."

He was wearing a robe and he looked down at his once mighty member.

"Yes," I responded in a low voice. This was not my proudest moment. "I just wanted to slow you down a bit so I could cum."

"And to make me squirt less so you wouldn't have to sleep in a wet spot."

I nodded. "The pink pill was for women. Faster orgasm and less ejaculate. But you took that one in the dark."

"But why am I humping out of control?"

"Because I used rabbits for my experiments. Apparently the results were a bit skewed for rabbits."

"So I fuck like a bunny and cum all over the place. Crap."

"You can say that again."

"Crap."

I didn't even bother to tell him to shut up.

We sat there and sipped.

Suddenly he brightened up, raised his head and chirped, "Want to have some sex?"

I reached across the table and slapped him.

"OW! What was that for?"

"You were getting horny."

"I was? Oh, no!"

And a few minutes later, he started to get that bright look in his eyes. "You want to make love?"

I stomped on his foot.

"OW! What was that for?"

"You were getting horny."

"Oh, fuck!"

Oh, fuck, indeed. I couldn't go through life abusing my husband every time he got horny. Well, I could, but I didn't want to. Heck, I liked screwing!

But if he screwed and shot his load he might shoot himself to death.

"What are we going to do?" he asked.

"Well, there is one possibility."

"What?"

"Take the blue pill." I looked at him balefully.

"But I don't like this pill thing. The last one...look how well it worked out!"

"Well, it's that or we tie your weenie to a pole and beat it."

"Beat me off?" he said, and I didn't notice how he was starting to cheer up.

"Just beat it. Or maybe I could hook up an electric shocker of some kind, shoot a thousand volts through your dick when you get amorous."

"Amorous. I like that word. Want to fuck?"

I looked at him, saw the gleam in his eye. Oh, crap." I leaned across and shoved a knuckle into his eyeball.

"OW! What was that for?" Then: "Oh. Was I getting..."

"You were."

He started to cry. "I can't live like this."

"Oh, shut up," I snapped. "You think it's any fun for me? I just wanted a kinder, more considerate man, and look what I got...Johnny Fuckemfaster."

He blinked. "I'm who?"

I slapped him again. He wasn't horny, but it was preventative...and

I sort of felt like it.

"Okay," I said.

"What?"

"Do you think you can keep your dick in check until I get back?"

"No! Where are going? I don't think so. I want to fuck right now in the worst possible way!"

I stomped his foot quickly. "I need to go get a blue pill."

"But what will it do to me?"

"Hopefully it will reverse the effects of the pink pill, but, honestly, I don't know."

"Well, I guess you can go…if you have to."

"Okay." I slapped him again for good measure, then grabbed my keys.

I made it to my car, then I heard that sound again.

"Eeeee!"

I rushed back into the house. He was just starting to squirt. Just standing there, legs spread, his little cock shooting out a stream.

I swung my leg and kicked him between the legs. I felt his balls all squooshy, then he collapsed on the floor.

"Thanks," he said. "I needed that."

"Well, crap." I said, sitting down.

"Yeah," he snuffled miserably, then crawled up on his own chair. "What are we going to do?

"Well, there's nothing else except…"

"What?"

"I'm going to have to take you with me."

"To work?"

"Where else? Yes, to work."

"Oh."

"I can't leave you alone, you'd probably just cum your brains out."

"Cum on my brains?" the idea looked vaguely interesting to him. I got ready to slap him again.

"Come on."

"Cum on?" his eyes were dazed, but he stood up.

I walked him out to the car and got him into the passenger seat.

"Where are we going?"

"To work."

"Wee! Take your husband to work day! Want to do a little of the old in and—OW!"

I had slammed the door on his hand, and not entirely by accident. Let the big goof think about that all the way to work.

We drove down the street, him sucking his fingers, and we only made it a couple of blocks. He took his fingers out of his mouth and asked, "Say, have we done it in a car lately?"

"Do you see that car over there?"

"Yes."

"Point at it."

He stuck his hand out the window and I raised the window.

"OW! OW!"

I rolled the window down and said, "Keep pointing. I may need to do this again." And again and again.

A few window roll ups later we turned into my company parking lot.

It was Saturday morning now, and the parking lot was empty, except for Martha Vanes' car and a couple of others. Now what the hell was that idiot doing here?

I got out of the car and went around to Jackson's side. I helped him out of the car.

He was getting weaker, and he was gleefully giddy. I was delivering more and more pain, and he was wanting sex more and faster.

God, wouldn't it be terrible if there was a correlation between sex and pain? Like what if me giving him a shot every time he got horny transfigured him? Made him want pain in place of an orgasm?

Well, hell.

"Hold your robe closed," I said, as I took his arm and began the walk to the front door.

He did, but I noticed that he was leaking. He was apparently building up quite a surplus of semen, and it was just drooling out of little clitoris-sized cock.

Curious, I reached into his robe and felt his balls. God! They were gigantic! I squeezed one experimentally and he squirted a big glob of semen out the front of his robe.

"Oh, fuck!" I whispered.

"That felt good." He looked at me. "You want to fuck?"

I made a fist and punched his balls. He squirted, but he also groaned in pain. "Shut up!" I hissed.

We were on the front walk now, just in front of the door, and the security guard was standing behind his station, staring at us with an open mouth.

I needed both hands to get my key card out of my purse, so I let go of Jackson. He was so dazed he kept walking. He splatted up against the window and raised both hands against the glass.

The guard blinked and was muttering something. He had apparently never seen a man, robe hanging open, spread eagled and naked and leaking cum against his front window.

I slid my card and pushed the door open , grabbed Jackson and we marched in.

"Mrs...Mrs..." the guard was so stunned he couldn't think of my name.

"Just a little after hours work."

"But...but..."

Suddenly, Martha Vanes stood up, and Jackson and I came close enough to see what was happening.

The guard's pants were down, his big shlong was sticking out, and Martha had been down on her knees slurping the thing.

"Judith?" she said hungrily.

Hungrily? What the fuck!

She came around the security desk and followed us down the hall to my lab. All the while she babbled, "I needed some...I needed...and the guard was there...but he's a man and I don't like men. Do you think we could..."

I whirled on her. "Did you take the pink pill?"

"Uh...I thought...it would help me...do you want to screw? Let me eat you? I give good orgasms."

She was close to me now and I punched her.

"OW! What was that for?"

Jackson looked up, "Hey...you want to make—"

"OW! What was that for?"

I grabbed both of their wrists and dragged down towards the lab.

I entered the lab, and Sandy was there, peering into a microscope. She looked up in surprise, "Judith?"

"Martha was leaning around behind me and pulled Jackson's robe apart.

"Ooh! A clit! Now this is a man I could love!"

"What's happening?"

"The pink pill. I gave it to the rabbits. And stupid Jackson took one, and apparently so did Martha."

"But...why? Don't they know how dangerous untested drugs can be?"

"Well, they're pretty stupid. Anyway, they're both horned out, and you have to fix them."

"I do?"

"Yes. Give them each a blue pill."

"But...but..."

"That should counter the effects of the pink pill, and maybe they'll return to normal." I glanced at them. Martha was down on her knees, sucking on Jackson's clit-sized peeny. "Whatever normal is."

Sandy went to the other lab and shorty returned with two blue pills. She gave me one and we pulled Martha and Jackson apart and made them swallow the pills.

"Now what?"

"Now we punch them if they start trying to fuck."

"Punch them?"

"Yes, we need to keep them apart. I don't know about Martha, but Jackson cums so much he gets weak and...and he might hurt himself."

"Oh."

So we sat down and began the watch.

First we had to bop Jackson.

Then, a short while later, we had to kick Martha.

Back and forth we went, discouraging their horniness as it arose.

"How long did it take for the pills to effect the rabbits?"

"An hour."

"Of course, a rabbit is faster than a man," I mused.

I left Sandy in charge of the horny people and powered up a computer. A quick search told me that a rabbit can run up to 45 MPH, and a man can run about 8 MPH.

"Hmmm," I stared into space. That meant a rabbit was five, almost six times faster than a human. So the blue pill should take effect in either six hours or ten minutes. Since they were both already on pills that might speed it up or slow it down appropriately. Hmmm.

"Eeeeee!"

I looked up.

Sandy came running back from the bathroom.

Jackson had Martha down and was humping her pussy, as well as he was able to with his short dick, and she was loving it and…and I kicked him off her.

"OW! What was that for?"

"I'm sorry! I just went to the bathroom."

I glared at my assistant. "Next time just piss in your panties."

"I'm sorry."

We got the two horn bunnies up and sitting apart from each other. They gave each other loving looks and I felt like barfing.

We sat there and I watched the clock.

Tick tick. For a bunny that would be 12 ticks for every 2 human ticks. When, oh when, was the blue pill going to take effect?

"This is sort of cool," Martha blurted, at one point.

"What's cool?" Sandy asked. I didn't care.

"Being all horny like this, and he's like the first man I ever met with the right sized dick."

"Oh," said Sandy.

I grunted.

"Unnhhh!" I looked over at Jackson. He was bent over.

"What's happening, Jackson?"

"I don't…know…I just feel…my balls."

"I think it's working," I whispered.

Martha: "What's working?"

"Shut up," I said.

Jackson fell on the floor, curled up on his side and held his little mini-weenie. "Oh…this hurts. Ow!"

We watched, and Jackson writhed and twisted, but at least he wasn't horny. And the droolings of semen stopped. His hands held himself and there was not a trace of his baby batter.

"What's happening?" asked Martha. "Can he fuck?"

"Shut up," I snapped.

"What about you?" she turned to Sandy. "Do you want to fuck? I eat a mean snatch!"

"Ew!" blurted Sandy. "Shut up!"

Martha looked at me hopefully, but one look from me and she shut up.

On the floor Jackson was huddled onto his face. He was all bent over and holding himself.

"Turn over, Jackson."

He stopped moving.

I jumped out of my chair and ran to him. I pushed his butt and he fell over. I moved his limbs out so he was laying spread-eagled. I put my ear to his chest.

Thup…thup…thup…his heart beat was normal.

I looked up and grinned, then stopped with the grin. Sandy had a horrified look on her face and she pointed at his groin. "LOOK!"

I looked at Jackson's crotch and blinked. His cock had returned to normal, and then some!

It was big and red and ugly, maybe eight inches long, and fat like dog that has been overfed.

"Oh…" he groaned.

Then his eyes opened, and his dick started to get hard.

Oh, fuck! It just grew and grew and grew! It was like a baseball bat! It was a monster! And his balls, they got big, too!

"Wha's happening?" He moaned, looking around.

"Oh, baby. You're happening!"

Martha pushed Sandy and myself to the side and jumped on Jackson.

I scrambled up and stared.

Old Martha the asshole was firmly impaled on Jackson's monster dick!

"Oh, yeah! Baby! This is better than pussy!" She moaned and began ripping her clothes off.

"Hey!" I tried to pull her off, but she was stuck to Jackson as if glued, and she waved her arms and brushed me off. Apparently the blue pill had given her a bit of male strength, and a male's appetite for sex.

"Holy fuck!" gulped Sandy. "What do you want to do."

I got up from where I had been so easily tossed and stared at the rutting duo.

Jackson lay there, not understanding, but at least not cumming out his ears. Martha rode his big pole, up and down, around and around, a gleeful expression on her old face.

"I don't know," I said.

"Maybe we should just leave them?"

"Maybe," I said, walking around and studying them.

Martha had her clothes off now, and she was pulling on her saggy tits, elongating the nipple.

Under her, Jackson writhed, but it looked like he was trying to get her off his body. Apparently he was tired of sex.

But was that the effect of recovering from his rabbit-like state, or was it the effect of the pills?

After all, the purpose of the pills was to slow him down a bit, and he definitely looked slowed.

Had I succeeded? Had I made a man who didn't squirt as fast and didn't have much cum?

It certainly appeared that way, though I would have to wait and measure his cum output. Which, the way he was looking around and trying to push Martha off, might be a while.

But Martha, she was still acting a bit rabbity. Did that mean—Jackson had taken ten minutes for the blue pill to take effect, Martha was still the same—would it take Martha hours to return to normal?

Then I had a dour thought. What if the blue pill only returned her so far. What if she was already imbalanced, being gay was actually an imbalance, and it only returned her to…what if she was, this was… normal for her?

What if her finally lusting after Jackson was what would have been normal behavior for her, after the pill had its effect?

"Quick," I snapped, "Get the camera set up."

"What are you going to do?"

"This is a scientific experiment. We need to record it. We need an accurate recounting of what is happening."

Quickly, Sandy set up the camera and began videoing the happy, lusting couple.

Well, she was happy. Jackson was sort of squirming and trying to figure out how to get out from under.

Sandy and I sat down in chairs with clipboards and we began taking notes.

"You know," I remarked at one point, "There is vast potential here."

"There is?"

"Of course. We can cure gay people."

"I didn't know they were sick."

"Oh, that doesn't matter, we can return them to what is considered normal."

"Whatever normal is," she observed.

"Yes," I agreed.

On the floor Jackson was trying to push backwards, but he just kept banging his head into walls and tables and things. On top of him Martha had pulled her breasts until they were pink and swollen. They might be a bit bruised from her pulls, but they looked like they were just hot and horny. She moaned and slammed her box on his giant cock.

"Please...please..." begged Jackson. But he was part of a scientific experiment, and outside of making him sign a release form I just observed him.

"Sort of hot," said Sandy.

Her eyes were glazed as she stared at the endless rutting.

"Hey!" I slapped her.

She yelped and rubbed her cheek, and at least had the decency to look a little embarrassed.

"I guess seeing all that fucking...it's sort of like a contact high."

"Hmm, we should look into that."

"What?"

"Contact highs. Let's say we get Jackson all horned up, and he has nowhere where to go. We could increase his pheromone level, excite the women around him. Maybe even give them a taste of the…the…Hey! What should we call our pills?"

We were silent for a moment, then Sandy came up with, "Super Rabbit Sex Pills."

"Sure. Give them a rabbit pill and they fuck like bunnies." I nodded thoughtfully.

"Of course we're going to have to adjust doses."

"And we're going to have to figure out the specifics of a man taking a pink pill to counter the blue one, or a woman taking a blue one to counter the pink one."

"We could cure people who don't like sex…"

"Or maybe cure people who like sex too much…"

"Maybe there's a market for human semen."

"You mean like selling it in gallons in the supermarket? Super good and healthy, vitamin enriched man milk?"

"Exactly!"

We sat there and thought, coming up with idea after idea. Food products, medicine, over the counter on the blackmarket through the dark web…the possibilities for marketing were endless.

"The good thing…"

"Yes?" Sandy looked at me.

"The good thing is that it is…people want to keep taking it."

"It's addictive…"

"Well, I'd be careful with that word, it's a bit negative for marketing."

"Oh."

"But people will want to take it and take it, and when they need to come down we can sell them the fast acting counter."

"Addiction…and a counter addiction!"

"Exactly! And we can charge people a dollar for the first pill, but a hundred dollars for the second pill."

"Wow! Sex really does sell, doesn't it!"

"You betcha."

On the floor it looked like Jackson was going to squirt. Martha was pounding away on him, Jackson had lurched his hips a couple of times, and I nudged Sandy. "Look, he's going to blow."

We watched silently as Jackson gave another couple of hip lurches, then he grunted, made a long wailing kind of grunt, and squirted.

"Quick! We need to measure him."

Working together we were able to dislodge Martha and knock her off Jackson.

Jackson groaned mightily, and I stared at his penis.

For a second I was worried. After all, when his penis was miniature he had shot gallons of jizz. What if he still shot gallons, and more gallons because his dick was even bigger!

Heck, if he shot a cup of jizz under the influence of the pink pill, he might shoot ten times that under the blue pill. And that would be all the blood in his body!

Jackson might die if he came!

Then Jackson pulsed his dick and squirted a single drop of semen.

Nothing more.

He was empty, and I sighed a sigh of relief.

Over in the corner Sandy kept hitting Martha, keeping her back so she couldn't jump on Jackson again.

So she might have lots of ejaculate, but it would take a while to find out. Apparently the blue pills were working, and Martha was now a slow comer.

"It's okay," I said, moving back from Jackson. "I got his measurement, now we need to get hers."

Sandy stepped back, stopped kicking Martha, and the old bat shot towards Jackson like a bat out of hell.

"No! No!" screamed Jackson, but it was too late. Martha was on him, clutching his dick, stuffing it into her dried up old pussy. I was really anxious to see how much ejaculate she would produce.

I made sure the camera was working and settled down for a long wait.

"Hello, honey, are you ready?"

Jackson was chained to a bed in the garage. It was his time of month. He stared at me with hungry eyes, he was drooling, from both mouth and cock.

I was wearing my flimsiest negligee. All made up. Pretty.

Not that it mattered to horny Jackson.

But I liked to look good. Girls always like to feel a little sexy.

We had finally settled on a once a month pill. Once a month he would get that good, old uncontrollable pecker. A big one, not like that shrunken weenie he had had during his initial pink pill.

For a few hours he would be filled with lust, ready to service, everything a sexed up woman could want.

I had taken my pill, and it was time to do my monthly duty.

Quite honestly, I wasn't all that interested in sex. I was making train loads of money from my line of pills, and I was interested in money.

But I gave Jackson a stipend, and he got to drive around in a fancy sports car, and do what he wanted while I made money.

And I didn't have to worry about him cheating because…he was on the pill. No interest in sex, especially with his limp and shrunken weenie, until I gave him his once a month pill.

Then he would get excited, uncontrollable, and I hoped once a month was enough for him because I sure didn't want to have to put out twice a month.

In fact, I was thinking of once every three months.

Standing in the garage, watching him pull at the chains, I loved him like this.

I walked over and stared down at him.

"Come on…come on!" He begged, rattling his manacles.

I through a leg over him and squatted, perched over his penis and spreading my labia.

"Uh! Uh! Come on!"

I lowered myself, and felt the delicious expansion of my hole as his giant cock filled it.

"Oh, fuck!" I whimpered. I think I'm addicted to big cocks.

I began to ride him then, and he thrust his pelvis up and tried to get more and more of me.

But he was so big I could only fit half the beautiful beast into me.

Up and down I went, slapping his chest and pulling on his nipples.

"Oh, yeah! Give it to me!" He howled.

But I could only give him half.

Still, it was enough for me. A few minutes later I sighed,

crescendoed, and fell forward. My tits smashed into his face, but I was off that big, beautiful cock. Hell, if I had fallen straight down, and taken that thing all the way, I would be destroyed.

"Huh! Huh! Fuck me!" He was piteous, begging, whining, trying to get me back on him again.

But I had had enough, and there was a huge glob of female ejaculate on his groin to prove it.

I stared at the mess on him, that was the reason I fucked him out here, in the garage. He would have a month to clean the mattress, or just get a new one, and the one in my bedroom would be fresh and unstained.

"Please, Judith! Get me off!"

I was feeling a bit sorry for the slob, or maybe just a little perverse, so I hooked up the electronic jacker to him. It was a tube that engulfed him, that went up and down and even gave little shocks to his balls. An hour of this and he would finally cum.

Yes, I had his dose down pretty good. He took a long time to cum, and when he did…just a drop.

The machine began to rattle and hum and clank, and I watched the tube go up and down on poor Jackson's over-sized cock. I smiled and placed the key to his hand cuffs on the chain around his neck.

He would cum, and start to be able to think, find the key and let himself loose.

And I would be free to spend a few hours talking with my lawyers and investment counselors.

I got dressed and walked out of the garage and out to my car.

Martha was waiting for me, she held the door open. "Good morning, ma'am."

Ah, yes. Sweet Martha was now my valet. The bitch who fucked my husband. The cunt who took my pill and transformed herself into a sex hungry monster and…fucked my husband.

Can you imagine that? Taking a pill for sex?

Who in their right mind would do that?

END **Full Length Books from Gropper Press**

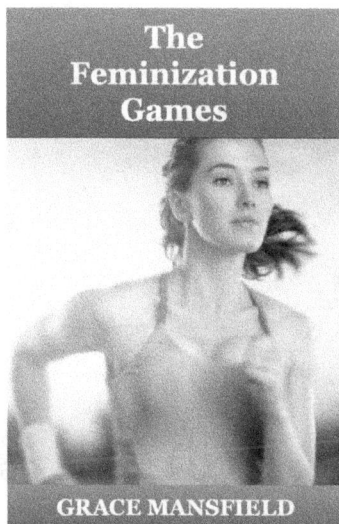

Jim Camden was a manly man, until the day he crossed his wife. Now he's in for a battle of the sexes, and if he loses…he has to dress like a woman for a week. But what he doesn't know is the depths of manipulation his wife will go to. Lois Camden, you see, is a woman about to break free, and if she has to step on her husband to do it…so be it. And Jim is about to learn that a woman unleashed is a man consumed.

The Feminization Games

Feminization All the Way

Male to female in a BIG way

PART ONE

"You have got to be kidding."

"I am not."

"Well, you're crazy then."

"I'm a woman who knows her mind."

"Well, you sure don;'t know mine."

Ronnie sat in the kitchen chair and stared at me. He's not a big man, rather slender, strong as all get out, but...not the manly macho look that people associate with manliness.

I got up, went to the cabinet and got down the Old Granddad. I half filled a glass with ice, then mixed equal portions of Coke and Granddad. I put in front of Ronnie.

He took the drink automatically, but just cradled it.

I sat down opposite him and waited.

"And you want me to...to dress like a sissy."

"And act like a sissy. And do work around the house like a sissy. And even wear some make up. And—"

"No."

He took a large gulp.

I studied my husbands face. "You have the greatest cheekbones, your hair is long enough to style, and you are going to have so-o-o much fun.

"I am so-o-o not going to do this." He took another drink.

"How can you say that? We haven't even talked about it."

He took another sip. Well, a gulp.

"This is my body."

"This is our marriage, and I can get an equal say in what you do with your body."

"No."

Bigger sip. Between my insistence and the alcohol I figured it would only take a couple of hours to break him down and make him amenable to my idea.

"But why would you want me to be a sissy?"

"One, you would look good. Two, you have the kind of body that lends itself to...to sissiness. Three, everybody I've talked to agrees with me. Four, there is something so delicious and wonderful about fixing yourself up. You are going to love it, and—"

"Who is everybody." Sip, sip, sip.

91

"Well, there's my mother…"

"Of course. Old Ironpants herself. The way she browbeats her husband…it's ridiculous. I would never accept being browbeated. Browbeaten."

Sip.

"Let me get you another drink," I picked up his empty glass and headed for the bourbon. "And I have no intention of 'brow beating' you."

"I'll bet that's what your mother told your father."

I put his second drink down in front of him and he quickly wrapped his hands around the glass and sipped.

"Besides, there is a huge difference between being brow beaten and learning to accept simple instructions."

"Instructions? That's what you call it?"

"Absolutely. And I'll tell you something else. Father likes it."

"I'll bet he does."

"There is something liberating about learning to follow instructions, in becoming man enough to submit to a strong personality, in learning your true place in the world.

Sip, hell. He was gulping.

DING DONG!

Ronnie blinked.

"I'll get it," I said, and headed for the front door. As I exited the kitchen I could actually feel his thoughts following me.

I opened the door.

"Barbara!" I greeted Ronnie's mother.

"Shiela, dear. You are as beautiful as ever."

We hugged briefly, and she asked, "Where's Ronnie."

Ronnie's mother is built like Ronnie. With large boobs, of course. She is also the height of fashion. Wears dresses to show off her fabulous figure, her hair is always done perfectly, and she walks like she rules the world.

We entered the kitchen.

"Good morning, Ronnie." She hugged him, eyed the whiskey and didn't say a thing.

"Good morning, mother." he sounded a bit disgruntled, but that was okay. Barbara was in on the situation. In fact, we had spent many long hours discussing how we could bring Ronnie to heel.

Barbara sat down opposite him and glared.

"What?" Ronnie protested. "I haven't done anything!"

"That's exactly right. You haven't. And it's high time you did."

"So you're in on this great plot to…to feminize me."

"I've always wanted another daughter, your sister always wanted a sister, and even Harold thinks it would be good for you."

"Dad does? Ha!"

Barbara took out her cell, pulled up a video and turned it towards Ronnie. On the little screen Harold sat behind his desk. He was a powerful man, thick in the shoulders, his grey hair cut to a short layer of bristles, and a grey mustache.

"Hey, Ronnie. Your mother told me what she planned, and I think it's a good idea. You've never been much of a man, and I think this will be good for you."

"What!" Ronnie squeaked.

"I want you to throw yourself whole heartedly into this, and I look forward to seeing the finished product. Good luck, " he hesitated..."daughter."

Ronnie stared at his mother. His beautiful eyes, so dark and mysterious, so perfect for a little eye shadow and mascara, were filled with shock. "No!" He whispered.

"Get him another drink, Shiela."

I was already on my way. I grabbed his glass, refilled the ice cubes, and half and half the Coke and bourbon.

"I can't believe...Dad's not a...sissy."

"Of course not. He's a manly man. Always has been and always will be. But Sissyhood is not for every one. It is for you."

"No."

I placed the glass in front of him. He almost inhaled the concoction. He was in such a hurry he actually drank one of the ice cubes. He bent forward and choked a bit.

Barbara smiled. "You can't even drink a drink like a man."

He put the glass down and glared at her.

"You will be much happier as one of us."

"I need to work."

"No, you don't. Your father supports his daughter...and he will support you as his other daughter."

I could see Ronnie taking that in, and it was true. His sister received a generous monthly allowance, and would do so as long as Harold was alive, and when he died she was on the will to receive a LARGE portion of his estate.

I could see Ronnie absorbing that.

"I don't want to," he finally said, shaking his head firmly.

"Well, hubbie dear," I quipped. "Looks like you don't have much choice."

"So you're going to make up my mind for me and make me."

Barbara and I looked at each. I shrugged and she chuckled.

"More or less," Barbara said.

"So you might just as well make it easier on yourself and go along with the program," I put in.

Ronnie finished his bourbon and Coke and stood up. "I think we're done here." He staggered a little, but he walked out with a firm step. Barbara and I looked at each other.

"Time for phase two, girl."

"I've got it," I said.

Phase two was simple. It was just me having fun. And the fun started the very next morning.

"Shiela? Where's my underwear?"

"It's all in the wash," I answered.

He stood at the dresser looking at his side of the drawer. Empty. "But there was underwear in here yesterday."

"I spilled some furniture polish on your stuff. It's all in the wash, so go ahead and grab some of mine."

He turned to me. "Oh, no," he said. "You aren't going to do that to me."

"What?" I asked, all innocence.

"Get me to wear your kinky underwear, call me a sissy, make me into a sissy."

"Oh, honey," I said, coming to him. I wasn't wearing much, just a bra and panties. I kissed him a good, lingering kiss. He wasn't about to fight that. "Just get over it."

"I'll pick up some more underwear tonight, and...no thanks."

He went to work commando style.

And was home an hour later. And well he should be. I had put itching powder in the crotch of all his pants.

He walked in, a little red-faced, scratching like mad.

"What's wrong? Commando not all it's knocked up to be?"

He just grimaced and headed for the shower.

While he showered I hid all my panties.

He got out of the shower, put on another pair of pants, was ready to head back to work...and started scratching.

"Son of a..." he muttered, holding his balls with one hand and scratching them fiercely.

Back into the shower. And out. And into my drawer.

"Honey?" he called. "Where's...uh, where's your underwear."

"What underwear?" I asked, coming back into the bedroom with a big smile.

"Your panty underwear," he grouched.

"Oh, that. You didn't want to wear panties. It might make you into a sissy. All the boys would laugh and try to pull your pants down to see your panties."

"All right. Knock it off. Just tell me."

"Well, I would, except..."

"Except what?"

"I don't just buy panties. I buy bra and panty sets."

He was blank.

"So you can't wear just a panty, or a bra, you have to wear them both."

"That's nonsense."

"Maybe it is for you, but at the end of the week when I only have a bra and no panty it's not so funny. At least not to me."

"Just give me the panties."

"Not unless you agree to wear the bra, too."

"I'm not wearing a bra!"

"Then you're not wearing panties."

He grunted, then turned to the dirty clothes.

"Wearing last weeks dirty shorts? How grody!"

"It's okay," he threw at me. "I just turn them inside out whenever they get dirty."

"Very funny, but still disgusting."

He started out the door and I yelled, "If you would get with the program you wouldn't even have to go to work!"

He just waved an arm at me without turning around.

That night I fixed him a big dinner, poured him some of that good, old Granddad, and wore a sexy dress.

Plunging neckline. My freshly shaved legs encased in sexy nylons. My reddest lipstick.

"What's the occasion?" he asked.

"Just feeling horny."

He grinned.

"And I like to get all sexy before I use my vibrator."

"What?" his eyes went wide.

"Sure. I've got a vibrator, and some other toys, and I feel like having a real girly orgasm tonight."

"But...but..."

"But why not your dick?" I raised my eyebrows.

He gulped and nodded.

"Because men are rough, and I feel like some soft loving. I feel like being made love to by a woman."

"A dildo isn't a woman!"

"No, but I'll use it like a woman should use a dick. Are you all done? Let me show you."

Oh, he was putty. I took his hand and led him into the bedroom. I placed the chair to my make up table next to the bed and sat him down.

He was blinking, there was a certain amount of confusion, and he watched.

I placed my dildo on the side of the bed, along with a butt plug and some nipple clamps.

He watched, and his mouth was actually hanging open a little bit. His eyes were dazed, as if somebody had actually slapped him upside the head.

I turned on the music and did a slow strip tease. I fondled my breasts, lifted them and sucked on the nipples. I could hear him gulping.

I lay back on the bed and reached for the butt plug. I greased it up and slid it up the poop chute with a big, sexy groan. "Oh, God, it feels good!" I writhed and twisted, then grabbed the nipple clamps. I set them on my nipples, and this time my groan was louder. "Heysoos," I whispered, "This shoots sex right to my pussy."

He had his hand on his groin. He was starting to rub his crotch.

I rubbed myself all over, squeezed my tits, then inserted the large dildo. Fuck, it felt good, widening me, rubbing all the important nerves.

"Honey," he gasped. "We could fuck…"

"I am fucking. I'm fucking my invisible girlfriend!"

"Your girlfriend seems to have a dick."

"Oh, God, yes. She does." I was pushing it in and pulling it out. My hips were twisting and giving little jerks.

"But…but…"

I smiled at him, a dreamy, half lidded smile, and picked up the little vibrator. It was only the size of a tube of lipstick, and I placed it on my clit. "Honey?" I asked. "Can you hold the dildo in place? Make sure it doesn't fall out? Maybe move it around a little?"

Like he was dreaming, he moved to the bed. He put his hand down and held the base of the vibrator.

"Yeah, now wiggle it a bit. circle it around and—OH! Yes…that's it!"

I began rubbing the second vibrator on my clit.

I felt the sensations, aided by his hand movements, rippling through my cunt. My clit was hard and I started to shake.

"Oh, fuck…oh, fuck…" I was losing it. I was losing awareness of him, I just wanted that big, deep explosion.

"Honey…"

"FU-U-U!" I groaned as the waves of vibrations hit me. I lifted my hips, pushing against the vibrator, and thank God he didn't lose hold of it.

"F-U-U-UCK! YE-E-ES! OHHHH!"

He stared at me as I spasmed uncontrollably. I bucked and arched and moaned so loud the cat jumped up and ran out of the room.

Then I collapsed. Just lay there, him still pumping the vibrator in and out of me.

I reached for his hand, caught his wrist. "Okay…okay…"

He pulled the vibrator out of me. "Take the…the…"

He detached the nipple clamps and I felt a whole new wave of sexuality ripple through me.

"Fuck," he muttered.

"Take the butt plug out."

He did, looking at it with fascination.

I smiled at him through half-lidded eyes. "And that's how a woman does it."

"I could do that."

"Ha. You're a stinky, sweaty, smelly man. I need a sweet smelling, gentle woman."

"You're just trying to get me to be a sissy."

"Is it working?"

He stood up and walked out, but he wasn't walking on a straight line.

The next day I managed to get him into panties. It actually wasn't hard, he didn't have much choice. So he glumly opened a pack and pulled the panties up.

"Oh, sexy." I observed.

"There's no pouch," he complained.

"I'll order you some sissy panties. They come with little pouches.

He didn't say anything, just put on his pants and left the room.

Barbara dropped by a couple of times over the weeks, and she brought him little presents. A negligee. A make up kit. A set of fake nails with bright, red polish.

"I'm not going to use that stuff. You might just as well forget about it."

She just smiled, patted his cheek, and ignored him.

Then there was the night I got him drunk. Real drunk. And while he slept the deep sleep I got out the nail kit that Barbara had brought him.

First, I pushed the bottom covers up and gave him a pedicure. Painted his pretty tootsies bright red.

Then I pulled one hand to the side of the bed and went to work. Nice, bright, polished, shiny, sexy nails. Stilettos. He was going to have trouble tying his shoes on the morrow.

And, the other hand.

Then, a little tired myself, but feeling very exulted, I went to sleep.

"What the fuck is this?"

I blinked blearily, then came to full wakefulness. His nails. Oh, my God! This was going to be good.

I sat up and looked at him. I wasn't wearing any underwear and my large breasts were on display. I was hoping to further distract him. Not that waking up with a full set of nails, top and bottom, isn't distractive enough.

He stood next to the bed and looked at his hands, looked at his feet, looked at his hands. "What the fuck did you do?"

"Why nothing! Don't you remember?"

"Remember what?" His voice was shrill, suspicious, and even angry. Poor boy.

"You were sleep walking last night. I went to bed, but you must have let your inner self do a little of the sleep walking."

"This is not funny!"

"I'm not laughing. I think it's cute. Beautiful, actually. Your hands are adorable."

"Where's the remover stuff?"

"I don't have any remover! Why would I have remover? I do my nails and I want them to stay. I imagine you would want the same."

"Come on!"

"Honey, honestly, I don't have any nail polish remover. I ran out and was going to pick some up this weekend."

He stared at me. Didn't believe me. But what could he do? Beat me? With those sexy hands?

"I need these off!" he was almost crying.

I slid out of bed and went to him. My breasts were almost against his chest and I handled his hands, turned them this way and that and admired them. I said, "Okay, I'll make you a deal."

"What deal?"

"If you wear these nails this weekend, just around the house, you don't have to go anywhere, I'll take them off on Sunday night."

"But I don't want to!"

"That's the deal. Otherwise you should just hop in the car and tool on down to the nail salon and buy some remover."

He started blinking, and tears were now coming out of his eyes.

I reached up and rubbed a tear away. "You are so beautiful when you cry."

"Honey…honey…" then he broke. He turned and walked out of the room.

I smiled. The bigger they are the harder they fall. Except in this case it was the more feminine they are the cuter it is when they fall.

That was an interesting weekend.

At first Ronnie wouldn't talk to me. He just grunted at my attempts at conversation, and turned away whenever I complimented him on his hands.

By dinner on Saturday, however, he was changing. But what else was he supposed to do? He had spent the whole day staring at his red nails. He had tried to trim the bushes outside, but he couldn't wear gloves with his nails, so there went the front yard. And he found that working the clippers with a full set of nails was…weird.

"You could always vacuum," I suggested. "That's easy to do when you have beautiful hands."

He didn't think that was funny, so he just gave up and came in and tried to watch football.

And kept looking down at his nails.

I brought him a drink and some popcorn, and I loved it when he picked up a piece of popcorn and found himself staring at the red tipped nails holding the kernel.

And putting the buttery stuff in his mouth was a whole new experience, feeling the nails with his lips, and licking the butter off his fingers.

Saturday night, and I hadn't done much but chuckle at his discomfiture. I asked, "How's it been."

"Fine," he groused.

"Different though. Yes?"

"Yes."

"Honey, I'm going to ask you to do something."

"What?" He didn't want to look at me. Poor boy was disgruntled and suspicious.

"I want you to hold up my hair, keep it back, while I suck your cock."

He blinked. Twice.

I knelt in front of him and worked his zipper. He took my hair in his hands, and I knew he was staring at the red lacquer amongst the gold strands.

"It's difficult just zipping and unzipping, isn't it."

"Yeah. Sort of."

"But you figure out how to use the pads of your fingers, and then it's sort of fun."

He was silent.

I pulled his penis out and licked my red lips.

He stared, aware of his hands, seeing his hands in my hair, as I began to bob my head back and forth on his hard cock.

"Fuck," he whispered.

I stopped for a moment. "Sexy. Makes you harder. Doesn't it?"

I didn't give him a chance to answer. I slurped and sucked, and I managed to pull his balls into the open and I massaged those.

He groaned.

"Don't these panties feel slick and sexy?"

"Come on," he whined.

"Admit it."

"I don't want to admit anything!"

I let go of his cock.

"Hey!"

"If you're not going to be honest with me I don't see how I can honestly suck your cock."

"I'm honest with you!"

"You are enjoying your nails, and you can't admit it. That's not being honest!"

"What does...I can't...you..."

I walked out of the room.

We went to bed, and I made sure I grabbed his cock with one hand. Shortly I was snoring, but, even asleep, I knew he wasn't. I knew how men reacted to sleeping in panties with red nails. He was lying awake. Wired. Staring at the ceiling and wondering what was happening to him.

He stirred, started to turn over, and I woke up and pulled him back. "Where you going?"

"Nowhere. I'm just getting comfortable."

"As long as you don't jack off."

"What?"

"I don't want you jacking off."

"But you do! You used that vibrator and—"

"Shhh," I placed a finger over his lips. "Women can jack off. If you were a woman, if you would just give up to the woman in yourself, you would understand that. Now, go to sleep."

I slept. He didn't. But he didn't jack off, either.

Sunday morning, and he had gotten a little sleep, but he had bags under his eyes.

I stretched and jumped out of bed. Fresh and rested. Naked. My boobs standing out and my skin fresh and glowing. I pulled on a negligee and went to fix breakfast.

A minute later he stumbled out, tired, exhausted, rubbing his eyes.

"Oh, you look tired." I looked up at him, concerned.

"I just need to cum."

Those big, black satchels under your eyes do not mean you need to cum. If anything, you don't need to cum."

"Come on, I don't..."

"Stay here." I ran into the bedroom, grabbed a vial and brought it out to the kitchen. I sat him down and unscrewed the vial.

"What's that?"

"Black bag remover."

"What?" he frowned.

I smoothed a bit of cream under his eyes.

"Is that make up?"

It's black bag remover. Actors and actresses use this stuff all the time. Go look in a mirror."

He left the room, looked in the hall mirror, and I heard him grunt. "What the hell."

He came back into the kitchen.

"That stuff will hide the darkness, and it has the added benefit of stretching the skin. Use it enough and it's like facelift in a bottle.

"You're kidding me!" he went to touch his under eyes and stopped. He felt his nails, looked at them, and put a grumpy look on his face and lowered his hands.

"Well, let's have some breakfast, then go out looking for garage sales."

"With these?" he held up his hands.

But the funny thing was that in sleeping with his claws he had become used to them. He wasn't showing the same reaction of disgust to them.

"Why not with those? I've got the same nails." I held up my hands.

"Hardee har har."

"Okay, look, I'll make you a deal."

"What kind of a deal? I don't—"

"I've got some gloves you can wear, and if you wear these gloves and go out to garage sales with me...I'll suck your cock tonight."

"Yeah, you sucked it already, and I didn't get to get off."

"You will tonight. In fact, I will give you a VERY special orgasm. It's gonna be short, but you'll want nothing more than to have that orgasm again and again."

"What?" he eyed me suspiciously.

"Word of honor. The gloves are in my golf bag. Go get them and try them on."

I fixed breakfast, and he was back in a flash. He was holding a pair of skin colored gloves.

"They're stretch gloves. Try them on."

The bacon was done so I took it out and poured the eggs into the skillet.

He looked at his gloved hands. "Well, son of a..."

"Told you. Nobody can see your nails, and yet you will have tactile abilities. Here, pick this up." I dropped a dime on the floor.

He looked at the dime, then knelt in front of me. Knelt, like a peasant kneels in front of the queen. He reached down and managed to close his nails over the dime and lift it. He looked up at me in delight. "Say..."

"Say," I interrupted and spread my negligee. "I need a little something."

He moved forward and I grabbed the back of his head and pulled him into my crotch.

Oh, God! It felt good. I groaned and tilted my hips, and his lips went to work. I could feel him chewing on my labia, then sucking on my clitoris.

I held his head and murmured, "Oh, my little man. Worship at my womanhood."

He glanced up, and there was confusion in his eyes. I pushed him back and said, "Of course you don't have to worship." I turned back to the eggs, which were about to burn.

He stayed for a long moment, looking at my backside, and I knew it was a very poignant moment for him. He had been in a submissive position, and he had liked it, and he didn't like being pushed away and denied.

Slowly, he got to his feet.

"Sit down," I chirped brightly. "Breakfast is ready."

I served him then, smiling and laughing, and he returned my attitude, but there was something else, a different attitude, hiding under his face.

We went to the garage sales, and he wore the gloves, and nobody noticed, which gave him sort of a kick.

We returned from one garage and he observed. "Nobody notices that I've got long, red nails."

"Nope. How does it feel?"

He hesitated.

"Go on, tell me the truth. "Well, it sort of makes me...hard."

"Pull over."

He pulled over and turned to me. I took his hands in mine and said, "You've been hard ever since we started pushing you, and I'll tell you this...as a woman you're going to be horny all the time."

I didn't say anything then, just watched him. I knew that deep things were happening inside his cranium.

He finally blurted, "But no woman is going to want to make love to a man who is...who is..."

"No woman?" I asked pointedly. "Or me?"

He stared at me.

"Because if you're wondering what other women will think, your mother, and my mother, and your father and your sister have all made it plain what we need and want for you. But if it's just me...you know what I want."

"You would want to make love to a sissy?"

"Honey, I want to share clothes and make up. I want to hold your hand in public. I want to go to bed and feel your woman's body penetrate me. I would even penetrate you."

"Penetrate…me?" he sounded dubious.

I ignored the place his mind was going and returned him to the idea of him being the dick bearer. "You've got a dick. Even if we go the hormone route we can choose drugs that will enable you to keep that big, delicious cock of yours. If that's what you want.

Man, I left the door wide open there. Hormones, penetration…it was a lot to think about.

I wondered whether he would go through that door, or whether it was too soon.

He was silent for a long time, just looking at me. I slipped his glove off one hand and felt his fingers, stroked them, felt his nails. I finally kissed his hand.

"I want you."

"But under your conditions."

"Definitely. But are my conditions that bad?"

"You're asking me to be less than a man."

"More than a man," I disagreed. "And let me ask you this…do actors wear make up? Do they have parts where they are women?"

"Well, uh…"

"And throughout history men have worn make up, war paint, if you will, and dresses."

"Kilts," he snorted.

"Take a look back through the Roman empire, and further. You will find men in skirts and dresses. Me asking you to be this kind of man is not far fetched."

I placed his hand on my chest, let him feeling my heart pounding under my breasts.

"I want you, in every way imaginable. But I need you to say yes."

We were frozen, but he couldn't make it…he couldn't make the decision.

Finally, he started the car up and we drove back home.

It was a lazy day, and surprisingly pleasant, especially after his resistance the day before. Heck, the weeks before.

We joked, we laughed. We watched TV and made fun of Sharknado. It was fun.

But in the back of it all was what we had talked about.

Behind our banter was a looming decision.

I knew he would make it. I knew he would give in. The only question was how much pain was he going to give himself before he did.

We got ready for bed, and I knew what he was thinking. He was thinking about that fabulous blow job I had promised him.

I got undressed and went to him.

"Lay on the edge of the bed," I said.

He rolled out form under the covers and onto the side of the bed. He watched me.

"Remember, this is going to be short, but it is going to leave you wanting this kind of blow job again and again and again. I can even see a day when this is going to be the only kind of sex you want."

He blinked. He was really wondering what I was going to do.

I took him in my mouth. I watched him, and he held my hair back. I bobbed up and down.

I wish I could say it was a long drawn out saga of sex, but he was horny, very horny, having not come for a couple of weeks, and having me play with him and tease him that whole time.

So it wasn't long before he started grunting and thrusting his hips.

I waited, made sure he was really going to squirt, then I pulled back and squeezed the base of his dick.

"AH...AH...PLEASE...LET GO!"

I didn't, and I resisted his attempts to loosen my grip.

He jerked and twitched, but only a couple of drops of semen leaked out of the slit on his cock.

"Fuck! Fuck!" He whimpered. his convulsions died down and I let go of him. I scooped up the little half a teaspoon full of semen and held it in front of his face.

"Do you want more?"

"Oh, God! Yes..."

"Good." I licked my fingers, and he watched the little bit of sperm disappear between my red lips. "Because we can do this...a lot...and there are a lot of other things we can do...if you're a sissy man."

"A sissy," he groaned, yet I could feel him breaking.

A sissy slave. Feminized. Made to do your will."

"Try it...you'll like it."

Then I pushed him to his side, crawled in next to him, and went to sleep.

PART TWO

That was the night that did it. That was the night Ronnie gave in to our way of thinking and came over to our side. But when he did make the break, the very next day, man, he went all the way.

"Hey, Dad, this is Ronnie. I'm thinking of doing this thing you and Mom want me to do, and I wanted to know if you'd support me."

I could hear the grumble of Harold's voice on the phone. Yes, he would support him...how much did he make at his job...good, I'll double that."

"Okay, I'm going to quit my job, so I'm depending on me."

"I'll go change my will today. And maybe I should send you ten grand right now, help make things easier."

"Thanks, Dad."

"No problem, and Ronnie?"

"Yeah?"

"You've always been a soft person. I think this is going to really work out for you."

"Thanks, Dad. Talk to you later."

Wow!

Second phone call. "Hey, Charlie? I'm going to be seeking employment elsewhere. Uh huh. No, I'd like to leave today. Yep. Okay. I'll come in and turn over my cases. Okay. Thanks, Charlie."

He turned to me. "I fired myself."

I found myself giggling. "How can you fire yourself."

"Well, I don't know. But I'll go in and turn over my work and be back by noon."

"Okay, I'll be ready for you."

He hesitated.

"What?"

"This is going to take some time. I need to come to grips with it, and I don't think I'm going to be wanting to be seen in public half transitioned. Is that okay with you?"

"Not a problem. You'll be my delicious, little secret. Now go to work and come home. I can't wait."

He went.

And came back at noon. Happy, whistling, and ready to go.

"Well, well," I greeted him with a kiss and a grope.

"Oh, God! Don't forget, I want what you gave me last night. Again and again and again."

"Oh, I've got a lot better than that planned."

"You do?"

"Sure. Have you ever been so horny you couldn't stand it?"

"Well, I've been pretty horny."

"It's going to be like that. I'm going to make you so fucking horny you can't stand it, and then, when you finally can't handle it any more… I'm going to push you over the edge."

"Wow."

"Now, come on, lover girl. Let's get you started on your big adventure."

He followed me into the bedroom and I opened some bags I had brought home just that morning.

"What's this?"

"Your own wardrobe, starting with underwear."

He held up a matching bra and panty. There was a bit of a pouch, not too big, on the panties. He stepped into them and pulled them up tight.

Perfect. his cock and balls were jammed into the pouch, his cock struggling to get erect, but there was re-enforcement and he couldn't.

"Little snug in there," he observed, but he wasn't complaining.

"Perfect. Now, take them off."

"But I just put them on!"

"But you didn't shave your legs."

"I have to shave my…oh."

"Well, we could use Nair. Would you like that?"

"Sure."

"Okay. Bottom drawer in the bathroom. Follow the directions and I'll see you in 15."

I turned away and left him to his ablutions.

20 Minutes later he was standing in the middle of the bedroom, putting on his panties. His legs were slick and smooth. I felt them and marveled. He always did have good skin.

"Now the bra."

I had to help him, men always get the bra inside out, but we made it, and I stepped back and admired him.

The panties and bra were a light blue, and they went perfectly with his olive skin color. I straightened his straps and he looked down disconsolately at his chest.

"I seem to have a little sagging material where I should have boobs."

"Not to worry," I went to another bag and took out some falsies.

"Oh, my!"

I helped him slip the falsies into his cups and he stared at the mirror. The transition was instantaneous. One second he was a manly rail. The next second he had curves.

"I really do have a…a softer body."

"You really do. And you've been fighting it this whole time."

He gave a heavy sigh. I couldn't tell what his emotions were, but he didn't stop or protest, so I guessed they were on the right side of good.

"Come here," we walked through the house to our own, little chat room, the kitchen. I poured him his favorite, Coke and bourbon, and poured myself a wine spritzer. We sat and looked at each other. We were both in bra and panties.

I reached forward and smoothed his hair, combed it down the sides of his face with my fingers and made it more feminine. He had thick, rich hair, and it was long, and I loved it.

"Ronnie?"

"Yes."

"Let's discuss hormones."

He said, "Gulp."

"I've investigated the matter, and estrogen will definitely soften you up, change your skin and give you boobs. Testosterone blockers will reduce your penis size, change the way you have sex and orgasms. I would think that we should go for the estrogen, maybe take it easy with the T blockers, and see if we can keep your dick functioning. What do you think of that?"

He hemmed and hawed, but it mostly just letting the concepts sink in. In the end we agreed, and agreed to watch his progress and make sure that no truly bad effects were experienced.

I didn't think he would agree so quickly, but, once in, all the way in.

We returned to the bedroom.

We put his first set of nylons on, and he marveled at how sleek and smooth they were. "It's like electric sex," he observed, at one point.

We decided on a simple house dress, and I gave him one of mine. It was silk and yellow and crossed in front, but not deep enough to reveal that he had falsies on.

Again, we looked in the mirror, and as we did I worked on his hair.

"God, I wished my hair was this thick and lustrous."

"I could cut it off and make you a wig."

"Don't tempt me," I giggled.

Then finally, we sat down at the make up table.

"Wow," he said, looking at al the potions and creams and powders. "You know what everything is for?"

"And so will you. Now shut your face and let me decorate it."

I did the standard job. I moisturized his face, washed out the pores and made it so his skin could breath.

Then I applied the primer and the foundation. Shortly his face had a smooth and seamless color to it.

Concealer, to hide the blemishes, which, fortunately, he didn't have many of.

A little blush to round his cheeks off, then the fun. The eyes.

I licked the mascara pencil and ran a line under his eyes. I creamed and powdered his eyelids, and he marveled at how smoky and mysterious they were.

And, finally, the cop de grace…lipstick.

Except I didn't use lipstick. I used lip stain.

"This will give your lips color for a long time, then you simply use a little gloss to bring it all out whenever you want.

He stared himself in the mirror. Transformed. His face made narrow and his eyes made large, his hair a delightful tumble of a mess, and his lips, I had used plumper, were rich and full.

And we were done.

We walked out to the kitchen and sat down to a couple of fresh drinks. I could tell his mind was in that far off place called thinking, and I watched him.

"It took us a couple of hours."

I was explaining things. When you figure it all out it need only take a couple of minutes.

"A couple of minutes," he mused. "That seems incredible."

I smiled. Women are incredible, and he was learning that from the ground up.

"Hold on," I said, "let me get something."

The something was my laptop, and we set it up on the kitchen table. Then we began searching through the various estrogens and T blockers. It was an education, and we spent a good amount of time looking at side effects, costs, times and so on.

And we joined a chat room and learned more. A lot more Here were the individual experiences, from the people who took the drugs, not just the people who wanted to sell the drugs.

And, finally, we ordered.

Done, sipping our drinks, Ronnie asked, "Now, about my boobs."

"What about your boobs?" I grinned.

"How big should they be?"

"Well, speaking as a well endowed woman, I would suggest as big as possible. I mean, we'll have to be careful, you need to build certain muscles, you'll have to always wear a good bra, but there is no joy like walking down the street and being stared at by men."

"Do you get stared at often?"

"All the time."

"I sort of noticed, but—"

"I really get stared at when I'm not with you. Then my whole body gets stared at, and I can even feel what part of my body is getting stared at."

"You're kidding!"

"No. You suddenly feel a prickly sensation, like hair raising, then you feel a warmth of attention, that's the only way I can describe it, on your boobs. Or your butt. Or whatever."

"Huh!"

I could see him thinking. "Don't want men staring at you?"

"Well, it is sort of offsetting. Underneath this feminine package there still beats the heart of a...a cock."

I laughed at that. "Well, no matter. You'll learn to enjoy it...yes, you will, and then you'll start to dress to pull it in, and you might even learn how to flirt."

He looked aghast.

"But it's always your choice. You can shut a man down, you can say no, you can run and hide...the options are yours."

He was silent for awhile, then: "But it's really just you I want to experience staring at me."

"Want to do something fun?"

"What? Are you changing the subject?"

"Yes and no. Now just lean forward, right there, and I'll lean forward."

We were inches from each other. Close enough to kiss. I could imagine our two red lipsticks meshing, mushing, turning us on.

"What now?"

"Now...don't kiss me. Get as close as possible, and don't kiss me. Don't let our lips touch."

We were eye to eye, breathing on each other, and I was getting so horny and excited.

He was, too. He was breathing harder, and gulping, and I knew...he wanted to lean forward, cross that final inch, and kiss me.

I reached out and put a hand on his chest. I held him back.

"Fuck," he whispered.

"Don't touch," I warned happily.

We sat there for a long couple of minutes, and our desire grew and grew. We were there, the purpose of 'there' was to kiss, and yet we didn't. I could feel my body heating up. Hell, I could feel the heat emanating off his body.

"How long do we do this?"

"Forever."

Another couple of minutes. The sensation of desire was so strong I could hardly stand it.

He jerked back and gasped for air. "I can't take it."

"Sissy," I said, and the import of the word hit him. We both blinked. then we both laughed.

"Yes, you are," I affirmed.

The days passed, and we entered into a new lifestyle, a new way of appreciating each other.

We got dressed in the morning, put on our make up, watched TV together, and even went shopping together.

Yes. Went shopping. He thought it was going to take a lot of time, but he could see that he looked like a woman, there was nothing to be embarrassed or scared about, so...there we went.

But it was the simple act of watching TV that gave us the most fun.

We would be entwined in each other's arms.

Sometimes I would cuddle up to him, lay my head against his chest, feel his fake boobs, and later on the smaller but growing real boobs, and we would just feel each others hearts pumping. Thump. Thump. Thump.

Sometimes he would lay on me, his head against my chest, like a little girl laying on her mother. Except he was no little girl, and I certainly wasn't a mother.

I think that gave him the most pleasure, because it was the first sign of him giving something up to me, of him being submissive to me.

Oh, he had a bad case of male-itis. He had mannerisms and ways of speaking and moving that were definitely male. But I worked with him, taught him how to walk, how to sit, how to be a girl. And slowly the male-isms drifted away.

"Honey, it's your turn to vacuum."

He turned to me, a beautiful woman in shiny black high heels. "Real woman don't do housework," he quoted from one of our favorite websites to me.

"Real women better, if they don't want a spanking."

He blinked, "A spanking?"

"You've come a long way, baby, but you still mouth off every once in a while, and we can't have that."

"We can't, eh?"

"No. Now, would you like to do your maidly duties? Or would you like to experience your first spanking?"

Now he was caught. He was becoming more and more subservient, and he knew it, but there was this spanking thing, sort of a step with finality, and we had talked about it, and here it was. Push had come to shove.

"Maybe...should we do it? Should you spank me?"

110

There was something breathless in his appeal.

"By all means. Now come with me."

I grabbed her wrist and tugged her through the house. She had lost some of her male muscle, and that and the fact that she was unbalanced on high heels, made it easy to pull her along.

We entered the bedroom and I pulled my make up chair out to the center of the room and sat in it. "Do you want a belt or a hair brush?"

"What? I don't want..." she was starting to realize that she wasn't in control. Excellent. She needed to know who was.

"Get me a belt."

"What? No!"

I grabbed her wrist and pulled hard, she flopped across my lap, wriggling and protesting.

I slapped her ass, hard.

"Ow! Stop it!"

SMACK! SMACK! SMACK! "You need to follow directions! Now you've made me angry! I would have given you a couple of playful smacks with a hair brush, or belt, but now you're going to get it!"

She started crying as I continued to slap her ass. She tried to get her hands in the way, but I was having none of that.

SMACK! SMACK! SMACK!

Now she was wailing, as I was wailing away. I knew her ass had to be red because my hand was getting red.

SMACK! SMACK! SMACK!

I kept spanking and spanking, and finally she stopped struggling. That was what I was waiting for, for her to give up resisting and accept what was happening.

"Get off," and she fell off my lap. She rubbed her fanny and kept sobbing.

"Come here."

She stared at me, frightened. She didn't move, however, and I tilted my head and raised a mean eyebrow.

She got to her feet.

"Come..."

I held my arms out.

That's when she understood. There is a time for punishment, and there is a time for forgiveness.

She knelt and put her arms around me. I could feel her body jerking as she cried, but she held on to me, wouldn't let go, and I brushed her hair.

"There , there. It's okay."

"I'm sorry!"

"I know you are. But it's all over now."

For long minutes she sobbed, then the tears started to fade.

I lifted her arms and she stood up, her head was bent and she still dripped an occasional tear.

"Now go do the vacuuming like a good girl."

She shuffled away, very defeated, and a moment later I heard the vacuum humming.

I looked at my hand. Ow! Next time I would have to make sure I used the belt.

It was months now, and her tits were getting bigger. I called her into my office.

My office. She was in charge of the pantry, and the cleaning closet. I was in charge of the computer and any business that had to be attended to.

Empty headed girls shouldn't be entrusted with business affairs.

"Yes, ma'am."

I smiled at her. "Ronnie, I want to talk about your breasts."

"Ma'am?"

"You said you wanted them large. Do you still feel that way?"

"Oh, yes, ma'am."

"Then I think we need to consider implants."

"Implants, ma'am?"

I sighed. Sometimes it was endearing when she just parroted me, sometimes it was irritating.

"Yes. Look here," I pointed to the computer.

She came closer and looked over my shoulder. I could see her reflection in the screen of the computer, and I loved it. She was so delicate, and beautiful. If somebody had told me she was a man, and I didn't know better, I would have laughed.

"What's this?"

"This is a model of a woman. It allows me to change breast size so you can better choose for yourself. I've chosen a body like yours, now watch…"

I rolled the mouse and the model on the screen grew larger breasts.

"Oh, my," Ronnie breathed, now fascinated.

"Do you want them this big?"

"Maybe a little bigger?"

"How about now?"

"Almost. Can we look one size larger?"

"Sure." I grew the girl on the screen and we stared at her boobs. She was slender, like Ronnie, but her boobs were definitely big. Probably an F.

"Is that big enough?" I asked.

"Well, my chest is still wider than…than a woman's, so is that going to be big enough?"

Well, that was interesting. My, little Ronnie had been doing her homework. She had been thinking about bigger breasts all along.

I turned the model, made her chest a little wider, then turned the view slowly 360.

"Oh, yes," Ronnie breathed, her beautifully made up eyes locked on the screen.

"Would you like me to arrange for implants of this size?"

"Oh, would you? Ma'am?"

"I think I shall. Okay, Ronnie, one more question."

I turned and faced her. She stood prim and proper.

"How are you doing?" A simple question, but lots of answers.

"I'm doing good."

"And the hormones?"

"I don't see any bad effects."

"Adverse effects." As she became more womanly she tended to become a little more air-headed. I wondered if this was engendered by her male viewpoint of what a woman is.

"Yes, ma'am. Adverse effects."

"And how about your penis?"

"My penis is fine."

"Is it smaller?"

"I think a little bit."

"But it still works?"

"Oh, yes, ma'am."

"Have you been jacking off again?"

She looked guilty.

"I've told you before I don't want you masturbating."

"I'm sorry, ma'am, but once you told me that women can masturbate, but men can't."

"Yes, women can masturbate, and they should. But if you are masturbating with your male part you are not masturbating like a woman."

"Oh," she looked stricken.

That was okay. I knew it was about time for phase eighty-seven, or whatever number we were on.

"Okay. I want you to not masturbate for two weeks, and then I'll show you how I want you to have sex after this."

Yes, ma'am."

"Okay, then—"

"Ma'am?"

I looked at her.

"Does this mean we're not going to be fucking anymore?"

I smiled. "Ronnie, you said 'fucking.' You know I don't appreciate it when you use bad language."

I thought she might object then, for I occasionally used bad language. So I snapped, "Would you like a spanking?"

"Oh, no, ma'am. Please, ma'am. No."

She was honestly contrite. I had only had to spank her a few times, but they were memorable.

"Okay, then. In answer to your question, I will be making love to you, but not in the accepted way."

Now she was curious. Very curious.

Yet she knew she had used up her allotment of questions. I was a patient taskmaster, and I answered freely, but enough was enough.

"Back to your duties now. I may have a visitor tonight."

Visitor. Code for a male friend. She hated it when men came to call, but I had needs. And I found that while I had wanted Ronnie's penis in the beginning, especially in conjunction with her very female body, now it wasn't enough.

Now I wanted a hard man to abuse me, spank me, hurt me in that way I liked so much.

Ronnie left to straighten up the house. She knew what would happen if she didn't have everything just perfect.

Two weeks passed, and Ronnie was on her best behavior. She had really blossomed as a maid, and she was now anticipating my every request.

"Herbal tea, Ronnie," and she already had it cooking on the stove.

"Bring my car around," and she already had it in the driveway.

I really loved my maid.

But it was two weeks, and I had promised, so the night was here.

We had dinner in the dining room. Well, I had dinner. A scrumptious roast, thick with sauce, potatoes with gobs of melted butter, and an expensive wine.

Ronnie stood by the side and waited for anything I might want.

"Delicious, girl."

"Thank you, ma'am."

I finished, and Ronnie began clearing the table.

"I've arranged for your new breasts next week."

"Oh, thank you, ma'am."

"Now, it's been two weeks, are you ready to make love the way a woman makes love?"

"Oh, yes, ma'am." Her eyes were wide, but certain. She had obviously been looking forward to this.

"Very well. You may do the dishes. Afterwards you may eat, or report to the playroom."

I loved it. She had a choice. No doubt she would be hungry, but this was her chance to have sex.

"Yes, ma'am."

Some 45 minutes later Ronnie reported to the playroom.

The playroom had once been our entertainment center, but I had collected a bunch of toys there and used it for sex.

Normally Ronnie stood outside the door, forced to listen as my lovers had their way for me. Tonight she was going to be in the room.

"Come in, Ronnie."

She entered the room and looked around. I had a new piece of furniture, amongst all the whips and dildos and various other toys, and she scrutinized it.

"This is my special bench. I ordered it just for you."

"Ma'am?"

It was like a sawhorse with a wide plank. There were cushions on the thing, and four platforms attached to the legs.

"Lay down, your head at this end."

She climbed up and lay down. Her head was slightly propped up, as was her butt. She had her knees and elbows on the four platforms, and I started fastening them in place.

Ronnie was starting to tremble. She had been spanked, but this was something new.

I fastened a belt over her back. Now she was immobile. All she could do was wiggle her butt and her head. And that not much.

"Comfortable?" I asked.

"Uh, yes, ma'am. I guess."

"Excellent. I'm going to have a drink before we get started. Would you like one?"

"Yes, ma'am." It sounded like there was a tremble in her voice. I had spanked her before, but here she was held motionless, helpless. Whatever was going to happen she would have no control over.

I went to the kitchen and mixed a couple of drinks. I returned to the playroom and sat cross legged next to her head. She could see me by turning her head, but just a little.

"Your make up is wonderful," I said, holding her glass for her.

She sipped through a straw and her eyes widened.

"You did so love your bourbon," I remarked.

"Yes, ma'am."

"I am very pleased with you. I know you had your doubts in the beginning, but admit it. You are living the life."

"Yes, ma'am," and there was a tone of immense gratitude in her voice.

"Do you like being a woman?"

"Oh, yes, ma'am."

"Do you like it when I make the decisions?"

"I do. It's…I do."

I nodded.

We were sipping away, and it was getting close to time.

"I know," I said with a sigh. "There is something so nice about not having to think or make decisions. When was the last time you made a decision?"

"This morning," she answered, actually surprising me. I didn't think she had made a decision for weeks. "You said I could fix sausage or bacon, and I really had to think about that before making a decision."

I nodded. Of course. "Did you like making that decision?"

"It was difficult." Meaning she didn't like it.

Our glasses were empty now, so it was time. I got to my feet. "All right, Ronnie. Are you ready?"

"Yes, ma'am."

I slapped her ass on the way to a cabinet. She jerked, no doubt thinking that a spanking was going to be part of her sexual experience.

Inside the cabinet was a dildo, but it was a very special dildo. It was bulbous, and the bulb hooked over, and it was more designed for prostate massage.

"I lubed up the prostate massager, then pushed a large glop of lube into her asshole.

"Oh!"

"Quiet," I swatted her ass, and she immediately bit her tongue.

I ran my hands over her round ass, pushed a finger in and began to spread the lube around, and to rim her asshole.

"Oh…oh!" She blurted.

I went to two fingers, made her happy for a while, then to three.

Now she was in nirvana, almost humming with the good feeling.

"Okay, my dear. Are you ready?"

"Yes, ma'am."

I put the prostate massager up to her button, I gently inserted it.

"Oh!" she gasped.

I swirled it around.

"Oh, oh!"

I lifted it slightly and began moving it up and down, up and down.

"Oh, my gosh," she sounded so happy.

I could feel her prostate, I began tapping it with the end of the prostate massager.

"Unh…oh…"

She began pushing her ass back, trying to fuck it.

"Don't move, sweetheart. Let me do all the work."

I took my time, and she relaxed, and then she blurted…"Oh…oh…"

"What's happening?"

"I feel so good! This is so good!"

I kept massaging her prostate.

"But I think I'm going to pee."

"Go right ahead. I put a bowl under you."

"But…a bowl isn't enough! It will splatter."

"That's okay. Let your little pee out." I spoke soothingly, and she responded wonderfully. I looked beneath her balls and saw the end of her small dick. White fluid was forming, seeping out of the slit and starting to elongate downwards.

"Oh, no!"

"It's okay. Go ahead and let your urine go."

And she finally did. For a long minute the semen poured out of her. Not in spurts, but a long stream. She sighed deeply.

"What's happening?"

"It just feels so good. It's warm, like an orgasm, but not so intense. It feels so gushy good.

I chuckled. Gushy good. I would have to remember that.

Finally, the stream of fluid slowed down, then stopped.

"Still feeling good?" I asked.

"Excellent," I pulled the prostate massager out of her.

"Hey! What are you…"

"That's all, honey. You're empty now."

"What do you mean I'm empty?"

"You have no more of that sticky mess in you."

I untied her and helped her stand up.

"Look under there."

She looked under the horse, and right under where her little penis had been there was a bowl filled with semen.

"I did that?"

"You did."

"But…but I didn't orgasm!"

"You're not supposed to. You're supposed to just get rid of your semen and feel gushy good."

"But…but…"

I shushed her with a finer to her red lips. "Honey, you've had your cum, and that's the way sex is supposed to be from now on."

"But I…but…"

"Did you want to get in me?"

"Well, I thought…"

"Honey, except for the odd occasion when I feel like experiencing a little penis, those days are over. But I'll milk you like this at least once a week. And here's the good part…"

She looked at me.

"Your balls are empty, but your mind is not. You're still going to be so deliciously horny. In fact, you can go jack off now. You will stroke and stroke, until your little cock is raw, but you won't be able to have an orgasm. You're going to be hornier than you have ever been. Isn't that wonderful?"

"Well, I....uh..."

"Now, be a dear and cleanup in here, then it's time for bed."

"But it's still early!"

"That's okay. Mommy has a visitor coming."

I walked out of the playroom. Behind me Ronnie picked up the bowl of her cum and made a face.

END

Full Length Books from Gropper Press

MY HUSBAND'S FUNNY BREASTS

It's not so funny when
it's happening to you!

GRACE MANSFIELD

Tom Dickson was a happy camper. He lived a good life, had a beautiful wife, then he started to grow breasts, his hair grew long, and his body reshaped. Now Tom is on the way to being a woman, and he doesn't know why.

This book has forced feminization, cross dressing, hormones, gender transformation, pegging and breast growth.

My Husband's Funny Breasts

Feminized for His Own Good!
Training Your Man to Love You!

PART ONE

"Oh, man," Tommy sighed. He was sitting on a lounge chair next to me, totally bored.

"What?" I asked.

We were both naked, the sun was out, and life was great. Or so I thought.

"I'm bored," he said.

"You weren't bored a half hour ago."

He smiled. No, he hadn't been bored. He had been ears deep in my pussy, gobbling it voraciously, sticking his fingers into me, putting his dick in me, suckling my tits like a maniac. No, he hadn't been bored then.

"Yeah, but that was then."

"You want to fuck again?" I grinned and hefted a boob at him hopefully.

"I'd love to, but…" He looked down at his dick. It was slack. Flaccid. Done. Empty. Not a bit of boner in it.

"Aw, poor boy," I laughed. "You ran out of hard. Too bad you're not like a woman. A hole never has to worry about being done. I mean, how can a hole be limp?"

"You're just making fun of me," he grouched.

"Yep," I said. "But, fun aside, I could do it again, right now. Probably even have an orgasm. You want to eat me right now?"

He glanced at me. "I think you're, uh, filled with sperm right now."

"Yeah, and poor Tommy doesn't want to eat a sperm filled pussy. Even though he wants me to suck the sperm right out of his cock."

"Different," He closed his eyes and tried to ignore me.

"Different because you've got different standards…double standards."

"Come on," he groused. "Leave me alone."

My voice tightened up a bit, and I snapped, "A half hour ago you didn't want me to leave you alone."

"A half hour ago I had the world's biggest boner."

"That little thing?"

He opened his eyes and looked at me. "I'm bored, and you're pissed. Which is worse?"

I sat up and glared at him. "I'll tell you what's worse…a half hour ago you were loving me, telling me how beautiful I am, telling me how you'd love me forever. Now you're bored, and you don't care about me. You're making me feel like a dish rag that's just been thrown away."

He grinned, "I'm a victim of my cock."

"Not yet," I snapped.

He frowned. "What does that mean?"

"It means that if the only way you can appreciate me is to be horny, then so be it."

"Oh, come on. You're taking this all out of context. It's no big deal."

"Sure, no big deal for you, but then you just got your rocks off."

"And so did you."

I didn't say anything.

He straightened up and started smiling. "You did, didn't you?"

I looked away.

"Oh, my God! That's what this is about. You didn't get your rocks off."

"Ladies don't have rocks," I stated haughtily.

"No, but you're pissed off because you're frustrated and you're taking it out on me, all because you didn't have an orgasm.

"You're an asshole, Tommy."

I stood up and he laughed. "Little Missy Pissy didn't squirt."

"A crude asshole," I walked into the house.

And he, in the male asshole mode, followed me, laughing and making fun of me. "Wanted to fuck but had no luck, yuckety yuckety yuck."

I spun on him, finally pissed. "Okay, lover boy. One month with no sex for you."

He blinked, then he laughed. "You're shitting me."

"You're not my favorite turd."

He just laughed some more. "Hell, you're going to be crying for it within a week."

I stared at him, then huffed off to the bedroom. I came out five minutes later, dressed and sexy and ready to go.

"Where you going?"

"To see Marsha."

"Oh, God. Chick talk. A hen party. I'll stay home and watch the game, thank you."

"Nobody asked you to come."

"No, but you will," he waggled his weenie at me.

"And you may as well get dressed," I snapped. "Being naked is going to do you no good for a month."

"I'll just jack off," he yelled at me as I closed the door.

He'd just jack off. Son of a bitch. And I knew he would.

Driving my Mustang over to Marsha's I tried to relax, but I was still pissed when she opened the door.

Marsha is a red head, a ginger, a few inches taller than me, and with a wicked sense of humor. I walked past her. "Hi girlfriend." I snarled, and I sat down on the couch facing outward. She lived in an apartment and we had a great view of the city.

"Uh oh," she quipped. "Somebody's got their tit in the wringer."

I snorted.

"Well, hold on. I'll get the cure."

A minute later she was back with a couple of glasses of wine. She sat down in the chair catty corner to me and we sipped and looked out over the city.

And, five minutes later, "You ready to talk?"

"I guess so."

She waited.

"It's Tommy. We made love, and it was good, then he started insulting me. Talked about being bored, then we started fighting, and I finally told him no sex for a month."

Marsha spurted a bit of wine out and started laughing. "You really told him that?"

"Darned right. Asshole shouldn't insult the girl he wants to…you know?"

"Believe me. I know. That's why I live alone. I get a booty call, then I kick them out. I can roll to the other side of the bed and avoid the wet spot, and I don't need to put up with their bullshit."

"Yeah," I said. "Bullshit."

"So are you going to do it? Close your legs on him for a month?"

"I want to."

She nodded. "Big difference between want to and can."

"Big," I agreed. I turned to her. "I just know that I'm going to get hungry and need a little, and then he's learned nothing, and…I don't know what to do."

"Well, if Tommy was *my* boyfriend…"

"What? What would you do?"

"Two things. First, I would buy the biggest and best vibrator on the market."

"Hell," I giggled. "I have one of those."

"And second…"

"Yes?"

"I'd make him wear a chastity tube."

"A what?"

"A chastity device. Goes around his cock, locks, makes it so he can't fuck, can't even get a hard on. Believe me, a month of that and you'll have a different boyfriend."

I giggled. "Won't that hurt him? I mean, don't men need to…to relieve the pressure?"

"Or what?" she quipped wryly, "Their balls will explode?"

"Well, I don't—"

"Listen, girlfriend, the only thing that is going to happen is that his balls will turn blue, and then his attitude will change, and then you will have a nice, polite, well manner boyfriend. A boyfriend who will pledge his love for you, will throw his coat over a mud puddle for you to walk on, with his body still in it."

We were laughing now, and she brought out the wine and we imbibed a bit more.

"But where do you get a…a chastity tube thingie?"

Marsha leaned forward and picked up her cell phone. She clicked the side button and asked, "Where do I buy a chastity device?"

Her phone answered, "Here's what I found." She turned the phone to me. Amazon. Wikipedia. An article on ancient chastity devices being a myth.

"Fuck," I said. I looked at her, "But how do I get him into one?"

"Hell, that's even easier. Just challenge his maleness. All men are proud and ready to fight, so challenge him. Bet him. And tell him it'll be the best cum of his life when you finally let him shoot."

"When I let him shoot…" I was awed. Me in charge of his penis. Wow.

For the next two hours we ransacked the net, looked for a secure device and giggled constantly. I was going to put my man in prison. And I would have the key. Wow!

Tommy was on better behavior the next two days. He only snickered a little bit, and he mockingly opened doors for me, and…underneath he was the same asshole.

Finally, on Wednesday evening, he began to ease up. The reason? He was horny.

Oh, yeah. Make fun of me for days, but when you want to get your rocks off…not this time, brother.

I left my bra and panties on before bed. I slipped under the covers, and his hand immediately caressed me.

"None of that, buster." I pushed his hand away.

"Come on, baby, you know you want it."

I spun over and faced him in the dark. "Tommy, you've been an asshole to me the last couple of days, but now you want something."

"Hey, I'm sorry. I was just joking and—"

"I want you to do something for me."

"What?"

"I want you to not make love to me for a month."

"Huh! That again."

"But I want to sweeten the pot."

"How?"

"I want you to wear a chastity tube."

"A what?"

"I explained that it was a kinky thing that couples used to spice up their sex life. I told him it would be good for us, and that he would get all horny and really love it, and that, when the month was over, he would have the greatest cum in the history of cums, in the history of sex, in the history of the universe.

"Well, I don't know. I mean, putting my junk in a cage? Isn't that a bit extreme?"

"Of course it is, and only a real man would be willing to do that, to prove himself, to test himself, to prepare him for an orgasm so powerful his toes might actually fall off."

He laughed, "My toes? They'd fall off?"

"So I've been told," I replied. "Maybe your fingers, too."

"And my nose and my ears," he was laughing at the idea.

"Maybe. But not your dick." I grabbed it under the covers. Hard. Made him gasp. "Your dick, when I let it out, will be twice as big, and it will shoot ten times the cum. You'll be so hard you could pound nails with the thing, and if you shoot your load into me you'll…you'll…" I was running out of words, but he supplied the analogy.

"It'll come out your asshole?"

Ew. Disgusting. But if that's what floats his boat. I squeezed his dick and kissed him hard, then said, "You'll cum so much it leaks out my asshole, my ears, my nose…"

"Every orifice," he blurted.

I blinked, what the fuck…is every man this sick?

"Every orifice," I confirmed.

He lay there, his mind alive with the possibilities.

I stroked his dick a bit.

"Well, I don't…"

So we sat there for an hour, me stroking and squeezing, and finally getting him close and backing off, and poor Tommy, being a man, he was prisoner to his dick. Which is to say his dick started doing all the thinking. And he finally said, "Okay. I'll do it."

I kissed him, sat on him, felt his dick throbbing between my cheeks.

"So let's have a little in and out right now. Just to get in the mood."

"To get in the mood for going without sex for a month you have to go without sex."

I laid down, rolled over, and went to sleep. And dreamed happy dreams of penises running through the fields, squirting blue flowers and singing, 'If I had a big fuck…la la la la la la!'

It took two days for the chastity tube to arrive, and those were a rough two days. Tommy was all over me. He had been denied, and it had made him even hornier. Made me wonder what he would be like after a month.

But I had to take my showers quickly, and get dressed quickly. I had to walk through a room fast, before he could get up and grab me. And when he did manage to grab me I was subjected to big, slobbery kisses, exclamations of love, and his eternally groping hands.

But, here's the weird thing, though it was irksome, there was a part of me that loved it.

Sure, I didn't like being held down and slobbered over. But it wasn't like he was mean…he was just…in love! He was horny. And for the first time in a long, long time, probably since he learned the difference between jacking off and fucking, he became a bit more polite.

Now that was an eye opener. Politeness. Because he wanted something. Hmm.

And, during that two days, when I wasn't fending off lover boy, I started reading up on chastity and other stuff. And the other stuff got *real* interesting.

Some women, it appeared, like to take their chastity bound men a little further. They liked to make them wear a little make up, dresses, and the men would prance about in maid uniforms.

Maid uniforms? Holy Phuk!

Women would actually do that?

And the men would let them?

But, as I read articles on everything from chastity to female domination to feminization, I began to understand. A man is driven by his dick. Well, of course he is. I knew that. But I didn't know to what extent.

I chatted with Marsha several times. We discussed what I was reading, and comparing it to what she already knew, and she gave me a tip that really helped.

"Go to Gropper Press, it's the best site for Feminization, and it covers a lot of topics. It'll dabble in BDSM, female domination, chastity, but its main focus is feminization."

So I did, and my eyes began to open. I began to devour stories about men gone bad and brought back into line, men trained to serve their wives, and this idea of feminization, it started to really intrigue me.

Make a man into a woman. I had never thought about that, and if I had I would have laughed, or been disgusted. But now, with my current situation, I wasn't laughing.

I was, in fact, getting…titillated.

it was hot to think of a man all dressed up, his skin shaved and smooth, wearing nylons and…and lipstick.

I started to dream of Tommy with his eyes shadowed and his lips plump and bright and so…so…kissable.

But I didn't want a woman!

But I did want something softer, but with a dick, who treated me as gently as…as a woman would.

DING DONG!

"I'll get it!" Tommy hurried for the door. He seemed to have more energy these days and I watched him scurry across the foyer. He opened, accepted something, and walked back in holding a small box. It was addressed to me.

"What's this?"

"I think it's your chastity tube."

"It's my…we're really going through with that?"

"If you ever want to squirt your little weenie again." I said it a little abruptly, and he stared at me.

"Come on," I grinned and tried to take some of the tenseness out of the moment. "Let's go put it on."

He followed me into the bedroom, but he was nervous. He wasn't joking and making fun of anything now. His face was rather solemn.

"Off with the drawers, big boy."

"Oh, now I'm big…after a week of you telling me I'm small."

"You know I was kidding. Now, off!"

He unbuckled and I pulled, and a second later he was standing there, naked, and I opened the box.

A box in the box. A black velvet bag in the second box, and I poured the contents out on the bed.

A tube, looking smaller than it did in the pictures I had ordered from.

"Crap! I'm supposed to get my junk in that?"

"Well, if you were soft."

"And I'm supposed to be soft after a week of you teasing me and denying me?"

I ignored the tube for a second and tried the rings around his cock and balls. "I think this one will work, when you get soft, of course."

"But first you have to get me soft." I looked at his grin and it was apparent what he had in mind.

"But that would waste the time we've already spent getting you horned up. You don't want to start the month from here."

He frowned. I don't think he wanted to start the month at all, and that meant I really better not let him squirt.

"Okay, I've been reading."

"A book?"

"Oh, shut up. I've been reading about this sort of thing, and we need to put a bag of peas on your cock."

"A bag of peas?" he looked confused.

"A frozen bag."

"Oh."

"Let's go." I gathered up the pieces of the device and went into the kitchen. Tommy followed along, his big cock bobbing and throbbing, looking a little concerned.

I put the device on the kitchen table, got a bag of peas from the freezer and told Tommy to put his cock on the table.

He stepped up and laid his big rod on the wood, and I placed the bag of peas on it. I squooshed it a bit so it wasn't just a board, but more form fitting, and then I made some drinks.

"Just stay there," I commanded as he squirmed and whined.

"But it's cold!"

"That's the idea." I poured ice, bourbon and Coke into two glasses. Tommy's favorite, and sometimes mine, a Coke high. I think if you put it in a tall glass it was called a Highball. I used the tall glasses and gave Tommy his highball.

He sipped appreciatively, and I have no doubt the cold liquid dribbling down his throat helped him deal with the peas trying to freeze his dick.

I sat down and waited.

Sipped.

Waited.

And his dick simply wouldn't go down.

"Son of a bitch!" I snapped. "How long do we have to wait?"

"Years," complained Tommy. "Can't we try something else?"

"Sure." I lifted up the bag of ice and slapped it on his pecker.

"OW!"

"Oh, shut up." I had a good grip on his cock and I stopped him from running.

"But that hurts!"

"It'll hurt more if I have to do it again. Now…get soft!"

And he did.

I grinned, took the bag away, placed the tube on his cock—it went on easy now that he was a raisin—put the ring in place, and popped the lock through the loop.

Click.

From the look on Tommy's face it was…

CLICK!

The cell door clanged shut and he was on death row.

Nah. just a simple click, and I grinned up at him. I held the key up so he could see it, then I put it on the gold chain I wear around my neck.

"Your cock is mine, lover boy. And you'd better toe the line."

"Hey…but…"

But I ignored him. I had read the books and stories, and I knew what to say, and what tone of voice to say it in. Everything I did, from here on out, was designed to do two things. One, let him know I was in charge, and, two, to make him horny.

The hornier he was the better.

It was time to start retraining my boy.

So nothing happened. Not that first day. It was too soon. From all that I had read I understood that there was one prime rule: he will only become your devoted worshiper, or slave, or prone to feminization, or whatever, if he wants to.

And why would he want to?

Because he needs to get his cock out of prison.

A man must associate getting his cock and having a cum with pleasing the woman. Period. It was that simple, and that complex.

So I kissed Tommy, made jokes, played with his imprisoned dick, and let him get used to a totally overwhelming sense of frustration.

He wanted to get his cock out and fuck me. So I kissed him, and complimented him, and promised that we would. Soon. Oh, but, BTW, could you help me do the laundry first?

Then, that chore done, he was ready to have a go with his weenie.

"Oh, honey!" I would croon, then I would get down on my knees and take a ball in my mouth, and then suck his nipple, and cup his buns and hug him fiercely…and…soon, baby. Soon we're going to squirt that big hunk of man meat all over the place. But, first, could you get those dirty dishes in the sink.

By that evening he was almost out of his mind. His cock was pressing against the cage so hard I was afraid it would bust it. He was drooling all over me, and I needed to calm him down.

I fed him (made him peel the potatoes, and he did it like he was a Samurai warrior doing a thousand cuts) and started plying him with alcohol.

We usually drank sparingly. Maybe we'd get tipsy at a party once a month, maybe a couple of beers on a hot afternoon, but now I let him have it. I fed him drink after drink, and he sucked it down, and by eight o'clock he was staggering around, singing lustily, and leering greedily at me.

Then he went to sleep. Just took his dick with him and passed out on the couch.

Snore. Snore.

Poor me. High and dry. No cock to pleasure my pussy.

Except…heh heh…I had my big, super industrial, king size vibrator.

He lay on the couch, sawing wood, cutting Zs, and I went to the chair catty corner to the couch. I moved it around to face him and took off my clothes. I began to saw that big puppy in and out.

Oh, God! It felt good! Did exactly what I wanted and when I wanted. My pussy was heating up, I was pulling on my tits, I was about to cum, and…suddenly…I had an idea.

I got up and went to Tommy. I shoved him over a bit and lay down next to him. I put the cell phone in one of those selfie sticks and began pleasuring myself all over.

Oh, God! This was even better. I could feel his hot skin, I could feel his heart pounding, and I leaned on him and vibrated away, shoved it in and out, pulled my tits. All the while taking a video on my cell phone. In and out! Round and round…oh, fuck…oh, fuck…

"AHHHHH!"

The cell phone picked it all up. It caught my back arching, the way my eyes widened. It showed me pulling on my tit and slapping my pussy. It showed me cumming really, *really* hard.

Done, I went back to catty corner chair and watched the video. Geez! I had just cum, and it was making me hot all over again.

Then, another idea, I sent it to Marsha.

Ten minutes later I got a reply.

'I want to do that. Please…please…puh-LEEZE!'

I started laughing. Tommy snored away, dead to the world, and suddenly I was bent over, busting a gut. I typed in, "Come on down!"

Ten minutes later Marsha knocked on the door. Man, she was all ready. She was wearing a robe with nothing underneath, and held a bag.

She looked at Tommy, snoring away, and grinned.

"What's with the bag?" I asked.

"So he doesn't recognize me. It'll drive him crazy!"

After we controlled our laughter, she told me to man her cell phone.

I held the little thing and stood back.

Marsha stripped her robe off and slid the bag over her head. She had cut two, little holes, and she sat down next to Tommy. I held the phone still, occasionally changed viewpoint, and watched the magic unfold.

First, she sucked his nipples, held his caged cock and sucked hard. Made big slurping sounds.

Then she went down on him, and managed to get his cock, cage and all, into her mouth. She grabbed his balls and squeezed and pulled.

Tommy moaned in his sleep.

She got up on him, rode him with her pussy, slapped his ass and acted like a cowgirl. She sat on his face. We almost lost it when he choked and gasped under her pussy. Then, the coup de grace, she lay down on him and began vibrating herself.

God this was hot. We were girlfriends, but I had never seen her, or any other, woman get off. I had never observed a woman having an orgasm, and it was incredible, and magnificent.

She poked herself for a while, and moaned, and played with her big tits. Then she began to do the old in and out seriously. She lurched and trembled and moaned, and suddenly, like a volcano blowing its top, she let loose with a wail.

"GAAHHH!...FUCK...FUCK...AHHH!"

Her pelvis shook and shivered, her hips lurched, and she actually started to ejaculate on Tommy.

I had heard of women cumming, having a big, old squirt of liquid, but I had never seen one, and it was magnificent. She yelped and shivered and squirted, then she collapsed.

Tommy was drenched. The bag was soaked. The whole damn couch looked like it had gone swimming!

She gave me a thumbs up, and I stopped the video.

Tommy slept on.

The next morning I awoke, stretched luxuriously, and considered how nice it was to have the whole bed to myself.

I mean, it's nice to have a warm body to cuddle with, but not all the time. Sometimes it was nice just to have all that space.

I got up and headed for the shower. I turned the hot water on and felt the steam sooth my body. God, it felt good.

I mean, yeah, sure, it's nice to shower with somebody else. But... but it's nice to have the shower to yourself. To not have to shift your position, to not have to scrub somebody's back, or sexual parts.

Hmm. I was liking this new mode of living.

I got out of the shower and dried myself off just in time. Tommy stumbled through the bedroom and into the bathroom. He tried to pee standing up, but couldn't. Pee squirted all over the place so he sat down. He held his head and sat and pee dribbled into the toilet.

I stood, leaning against the door jamb, and asked, "What's going on?"

"I don't know," he mumbled. He was badly hung over. "My dick hurts. It's all hard and..." he trailed off. Too miserable to talk.

He looked up at me. "What the fuck happened last night?"

"Why, what do you mean?"

"I woke up out on the couch, I've got some sticky stuff all over me, and the whole couch is damp! Oh, God. My head hurts."

"Well," I considered how much to tell him, "I tried to make love to you, but you...you refused."

"What? No way! Ohhh!"

"Are you going to puck?"

"No...no...I wouldn't...Oooh, fuck!"

He hoped off the toilet and spun around and started calling for Ralph.

"Ra-a-alph! Ra-a-alph!"

The toilet filled up with a disgusting smell.

"Gah!" I said. I held my nose and turned away.

Fifteen minutes later he was clean and sitting at the kitchen table. He looked a little green, and I fed him some toast.

"If you can keep it down I'll make you some more."

"Oh."

I watched him, and kept my grin inside. Poor boy. But if he thought he was suffering now, he hadn't seen nuttin'!

A half hour later, him recovering somewhat, but still too sick to feel amorous, in spite of the way his dick was trying and failing to get hard, I sat down opposite him and shoved the cell phone across the table.

He looked at it and didn't move for a minute, then he blinked and figured out the opening picture. Him, naked, couch.

He reached for the phone and began watching the video.

Me on the chair, playing with myself, diddling myself, and finally having a grand and glorious cum.

"Oh, fuck!" he whispered.

I looked down. His dick was struggling in the cage. Dick willing, but stomach trying to throw up.

He looked up at me. "You…you…"

I shrugged. "I was willing. I had the key ready to go. You saw me hold it to the lock, but when you just snored…what was I supposed to do."

"You could have woken me up!"

"Honey, an atom bomb wouldn't have woken you up."

"But I could have…I'm so horny…I—"

"Want to do it now?"

"Ohhh!" he groaned. "I want to…"

"But you might throw up on me. No thanks."

"But…but…" he started watching the phone again, his dick throbbed, and he gulped rapidly.

I was going to draw this out, save the second video for another time, but he was in the perfect position right now. I decided, "Honey, there's another video."

"What?" his forehead furrowed and he blinked several times.

"Yes. Apparently you had a lot more fun than you thought."

"I…did? I did? What—"

"Here," I took the cell phone and started the second video.

A naked woman, with a bag over her head, laid on him. And played with him. When she managed to get his whole, caged cock into her mouth I thought he was going to curl up and die.

"Who?" he asked. "Who?"

"Oh, I don't know. I don't know who was under the bag."

"You know…"

"I just know that after I had my most delightful cum I heard a knock at the door. I opened it up and a naked woman with a bag over her head danced in. I guess she was passing by and saw through our front window. She danced around, rubbed you up and down trying to get a reaction—maybe she wanted a nice fuck—then, when you wouldn't respond, she… played with you."

"She got my whole cock in her mouth! With the cage!"

"Oh, yeah. Did that feel good?"

"How would I know!" he yelled. "I was unconscious!"

"Too bad. So sad. Maybe if you weren't such a drunken lout you could have gotten fucked. Twice. Did you see how big her tits were?

Tommy began to cry. Actually cry.

And I began to exult. Only one day. Less than a day, and he was already succumbing.

This was going to be easy!

PART TWO

Tommy cleaned the house…and begged. Tommy made dinner and did the dishes…and begged. Tommy threatened to break the chastity tube and jack off.

"Well, if you can't keep your word. If you can't be a man…"

"What's manly about having your cock locked up?"

"It's manly because it turns me on. It makes me wet. Do you want me to be horny for you?"

"Well…" I could see him thinking about it. Too horny, get out of cage, wife horny, stay in cage.

"But I just need a little relief! My balls are blue! My cock won't stop trying to…trying to…get hard."

"Yeah, but when I do let it out it's going to make up for all the deprivation. It's going to get so hard you could cut diamonds!"

"But…but…"

And so the arguments went.

In truth, though, he was enjoying it.

He was protesting, he was going down hard, but he was enjoying it. What man wouldn't want his whole existence revolving around and focusing on his cock?

But I knew that if I pushed him too hard it wasn't going to be fun, and I had to make it fun to win.

So a week went by, and I never missed an opportunity to play with him, to massage him, to kiss him…but it was time.

But, of course, I had a plan.

"Honey, you've been wanting relief. Are you still wanting?"

He looked up from the sink where he was washing dishes. He was wearing a pink apron, so cute, but it was mine, and he would need his own apron. His own set of clothes, for that matter.

"Does Godzilla want to step on Tokyo?"

"Then tonight, if you're a good boy, I will give you a 'little' relief."

He looked at me with his brow furrowed. "What do you mean a 'little?'

"You'll have to find out. But there are several conditions if we are going to make this happen."

He wiped his hands off and turned to me. "What kind of conditions?"

"Oh, a whole bunch. And you will find out about them tonight, if you want to get your relief. But, one condition right now…take off your clothes."

I didn't need to repeat myself on that one. He tossed the apron onto a chair and slipped out of his shirt and pants. He stood there, a manly man with his cock in a cage.

Fuck. I wanted to cum right then.

I picked up the apron and tossed it to him. "You can wear this. And I'll be getting you another one, one more fitting to your station. And I'll be getting you some other clothes, too."

He looked at the apron, I thought he might refuse, but he put it on. He wasn't done with the dishes, after all.

"What kind of clothes?"

"Finish the dishes and I'll show you."

Frowning, a little worried, he turned back to the dishes. I headed for the computer to pull up a few websites.

"I'm not wearing that!"

We wearing sitting in front of my computer looking at 'Janet's Closet.' Precisely, we were looking at bras and panties.

"Why not?"

"Maybe you haven't noticed, I'm a man. Nothing up here!" He slapped his pectorals.

"Oh, we can fix that," I clicked to the breast form section, "Choose your boob."

He blinked. He was resistant. He was even a little angry, but his little cock was squirming and wiggling and trying to get hard int he worst possible way.

He turned to me. "Why are you doing this to me?"

"Because you want it." I put my hand on his cage. "You can protest all you want, but your little cock is throbbing."

"It's throbbing because it's trying to get loose!"

"And it might get loose tonight."

"Might?"

"Whether you get a 'little' relief is up to you. And all you have to do is tell me what you would like to wear."

"This is crazy."

"Just around the house. Kinky stuff that will make me really horny. Nobody needs to know." I kept a straight face and hid my lie.

"But…why does it make you horny?" He was actually really curious. Not just protesting. That was a good sign.

"Doesn't seeing a woman in underwear make you horny?"

"Well, yeah, but—"

"Well seeing men in sexy underwear does it for me. Believe me, if you knew how wet I was right now you would jump into my underwear and run down the street jumping for joy."

He smiled at my words, good sign, but then he frowned. "Well, I don't—"

I spun my chair towards him, reached over and turned his chair towards me. We were face to face. I was wearing slacks and a blouse and full underwear underneath. He was naked. I reached for his groin and cupped his package in my hands. God, it was hot!

"Honey?"

"What?"

I leaned forward slowly. He was getting so weirded out that he almost backed up, but my hands on his groin, my red lips closing in on him…I touched my lips to his. I reached around and grabbed the back of his head.

For a long minute our mouths were attached, our flesh was heating up, I could feel the blood surging in his poor, caged cock.

I backed off an inch.

He stared at me.

I let go of his head and grabbed one of his nipples. I pulled on his nipples and his package and we kissed again.

"Mmmm," he groaned as I lightly twisted his nipple. I knew the sensations were shooting down to his crotch.

I took a long time, just making out, and he didn't resist. He couldn't resist. No man can resist.

I broke from him. We were breathing heavily. I said, "Pick your bra and panties."

We turned back towards Janet's Closet, and he kept side glancing at me. But, finally, I had his attention on the site, and he looked, and, finally…"That one."

"Excellent. I'm going to get you a couple of other things to go along with it, but don't worry. I've got excellent taste. Now, time to do the laundry?"

"Well, but I…"

"Go on, now. You'll have all day to anticipate tonight, and these things will be delivered in a few days. You are going to be so hot."

I patted his bare thigh.

He didn't want to get up. He wanted to stay and make out, and he would have even ordered more stuff. But I had pushed him enough for one day.

He finally stood up and went to start the laundry.

"Finish the dishes and I'll go get ready."

He nodded, and gulped. He had been thinking about this all day. He was going to get free. He was going to get to use his dick. He was going to…do what I told him to.

Fifteen minutes later he trotted into the bedroom. That's right. Trotted. Not walked. He was so anxious his skin was actually glowing pink. He was so excited his blood was surging through his body.

He looked at the bed.

It was a poster bed, and four of his neckties looped around the posts. I would get some handcuffs or manacles or leather straps later, but right now, he stared at the neckties and his mind started to blow.

"What is this?"

"It's a 'little' relief. Of course if you'd rather not climb onto the bed..."

"No...uh, no. I'm fine. He laid on the bed and I started fastening him down.

"I thought you were going to be naked," he stared at my breast as I leaned over him.

I finished the tie and told him to struggle. He struggled half heartedly. He didn't really want to get away.

"Go on, really try."

So he did, and it was obvious that he wasn't going anywhere.

"Okay, now then, we have a few rules to talk about."

"Rules?"

"First, I am going to go in the bathroom and put on my uniform. You see, lover dear, you've been getting entirely too excited these past few days, and it's bad for you to see my naked body."

"It is?" he was staring at me like he had X-ray vision.

"Yes. We need to calm you down. We don't want this," I grabbed his cage, "To struggle and hurt itself. So you need to calm down."

My actions, of course, made him hornier than ever. To be told he could no longer see my body, to deprive him, in his mind, was making him want all the harder.

"So outside of a few times, like when I need a massage, or for you to scrub me in the shower, you aren't going to be seeing my naked form anymore."

"I'm not?" he was gulping frantically, his eyes looked so wide and scared.

"But I want you naked all the time. Except for your cute apron, or maybe when I want to see you wearing something sexy."

"But, I don't—"

"Hush, dear," I placed my finger on his lips. "Tomorrow you will move all your male clothes out to the laundry room in the garage. When you have to leave the house you may dress or undress in there. Understood."

"Well, I..."

"Don't disappoint me now." I shook his cage. "I don't want to be disappointed. Do you want to disappoint me?"

He shook his head in the negative.

"Excellent. Are you ready for your little cum?"

"Yes." He nodded frantically. Poor boy. His dick really was doing his thinking for him. I looked down at it and it was actually drooling. Man, he was ready.

I went into the bathroom.

I didn't have a leather outfit that the books recommended, but I put on black underwear, pulled my hair back in a top pony tail, and painted my lips red. Finally, I put on high heels, I did have some sexy semi-boots with high spikes, and I walked back into the bedroom.

"Oh...my...God!" He blurted.

I sashayed over to him with a smile. He stared at me, couldn't take his eyes off me. I leaned forward, my hair brushing over his groin, and put the key into the lock and twisted. The lock came loose and I took the tube off.

SPROING!

He was instantly standing up harder than a gravestone!

I smiled at him, and took the beast in my hand.

"Take off the ring," he suggested, quite desperately.

"No. I like it when the flow of blood is restricted. I was hoping we might give you a smaller ring."

He made a moaning sound.

I started to stroke his cock.

There is an art to stroking the cock. You don't just jack it desperately, frantically, you must do it slowly, lovingly, giving the man no chance to do anything but feel it.

I laid down between his legs, he had a pillow under his head and he could watch me.

I put my red lips over the head and began to suck.

His eyes were locked on me, on my mouth.

I licked the underhead. I palpated his balls. I stroked him.

Slowly.

Within a minute he was groaning.

"Please...please...do me!"

"I am, lover boy. Now, did you want me to stop so we could discuss this? Or do you trust that I am a cocksucking expert who knows what she is doing?"

"I...I trust." He could hardly speak, he was so excited.

I stroked him up and down, I took him in my mouth again. I kissed under the skull, I licked up his shaft.

He began to twitch and jerk, so I stopped. "You must hold still. Don't try to fuck my mouth. That would be very disrespectful. Do you understand?"

"Yes! Yes!"

He tried to hold still, and was pretty successful.

I went back to licking his cock, kissing it, stroking it, and slobbering all over the head. I backed off and blow on the now EXTREMELY sensitive head.

He was jerking uncontrollably, but trying to hold himself still. It was so fun so watch him in this predicament. Sometimes I backed off just to scare him.

Finally, he was getting close. It takes a long time, maybe 10 or 12 minutes, to get a guy off this way, but the good news is that when he is close he doesn't so much explode as drool.

"Oh, God! Oh, God!" He moaned, and just as he started to surge, I could feel his sperm pulsing up the shaft, I backed off and squeezed the base of his cock.

"Fuck!" He yelled, and he tried to lurch and jerk free from my hand.

Nope. And a single drop of sperm oozed out of his slit.

"Let me go! Let me go!"

I just smiled, and his penis throbbed, and when the lurching was done, I kissed him tenderly. Then I washed him gently with a soft wash cloth and got him ready for the tube. He was already starting to go limp.

"Why did you...why?"

"Honey," I explained patiently. "You just got a 'little' cum. Was it good?"

"It was...frustrating!"

"Are you saying you didn't like it? That I shouldn't even give you a 'little' cum?"

"No...I don't...no..."

He was so delightfully confused. He wanted a big cum, and he was afraid to say he didn't want a little cum. He was scared it might mean no cums."

I slipped the tube on him and locked it with that wonderful

CLICK!

He stared at his cock.

"Do you feel relieved?"

"Well, uh...yes." But he didn't. I mean, he did, he had cum, and the desire was diminished, but...he still had a sackful of semen in him.

"Excellent. Be a good boy all week and maybe we can do that again."

I undid his ties, let him loose, and sat on the bed and waited. It didn't take long.

He embraced me, held me in his arms, and cried.

"There, there," I said. "You're a good boy."

He snuffled and sobbed, and slowly stopped crying.

"Now go wash the car or something."

"But…but I really wanted to fuck you."

"Oh, those days are past. But you can, if you wish, get me off."

"What?"

"Well, I got you off. Isn't it only right that you get me off?"

"But…I…"

"Of course, if you don't want to…"

"But I thought I wasn't supposed to see your naked body?"

"Oh, we can fix that. Did you want to make me cum?"

He nodded, his face was so tortured and cute.

"Very well, put this on."

I took a mask out of my bottom drawer. It was like a Zorro mask, but without the eyeholes.

Dutifully, he slipped the mask on. It covered his eyes perfectly.

"Can you see anything."

"No."

"Very well. I'm going to take my clothes off, but if you peek I won't be giving you any kind of cum for a long…long…LONG time. Do you understand?"

"Yes," he nodded.

I took my clothes off and lay on the bed. I spread my legs and said, "I'm on the bed waiting."

He felt the bed, crept across it, and felt my body. He felt my breasts, and I could almost hear his heart pounding.

"Suck my tits."

"Oh, yes!" he was so eager. He had just cum, but he still had a load of cum, and the excitement that went along with being fully loaded.

He put mouth to my breasts and one hand snaked down to my pussy. He sucked, and he tickled my clitoris.

"Oh, yes." I said. "You're a good pussy slave."

He redoubled his efforts, as if my simple compliment had inspired him.

Finally, I pushed his face down to my crotch and he began eating. His fingers were under his chin and pointed into my sacred hole. He was breathing frantically as he jacked my hole.

"Oh, yes…" I sighed, and my hips started to move. And I realized: *there is nothing like a blind man eating your pussy! There is nothing like dominating a man and having him attend to you in this most perfect manner.*

I began to lurch, to tilt my pelvis. I fucked his fingers and his face, and where his cum had been a 'little' one, mine was big, really…really… REALLY big!

I locked up in huge spasm, and squirts of clear liquid shot all over his face. My thighs clamped on the sides of his head, but he kept his tongue working.

"OH…OH…Oh…!"

And, finally, I came down.

He slowed down. I had no doubt that his jaw was aching.

I pushed his head away. "Now, go. Close the door on your way out, then take the mask out."

He slid off the bed and stumbled towards the door. I almost giggled, watching him feel his way around.

Then he shut the door and I was left alone. Feeling so deliciously wicked and good. And I wondered: *can I get myself off again? With my big vibrator?*

I answered that question a few minutes later, and it was a good answer.

His bra and panties arrived, along with a flowing negligee. I immediately had him put everything on. Heck, it was easy. The poor boy was naked, and loved it, but he wanted some kind of covering. I watched him as he moved around the house, doing his chores and getting used to wearing his new apparel.

And he loved it! Oh, it took a few hours, but he started moving differently, actually prancing and flouncing about. And I knew it was time for the next step.

"Tommy?" I called.

"What?"

He hurried into the bedroom. I admired his shape, so sexy, but he needed curves.

"I'm going to order you some hormones."

"Hormones?" He frowned. "What for?"

"You need to fill out your bra. And I want to get you a bigger bra to fill out."

"Oh," he was thinking about that. But, having already adapted to so much, he was almost accepting it all. Then he asked, "But won't that make my dick go limp?"

"Oh, honey," I patted his cheek. "You shouldn't worry about that. We'll just give you a lot of estrogen, but we won't bother with the testosterone blockers."

"And that will make sure I still get erections?"

I loved it. He was almost embarrassed by saying the word erection. My little Tommy was definitely changing.

"Absolutely. Some day I'm going to want to fuck that dick of yours."

"Really?" Instant eagerness.

"Sure. In fact, now I've got you here…would you like me to give you a good fuck?"

His heart almost leaped out of his chest. "Oh, yes!" I was pleased by how eager he was.

"Well, I could probably do that, but you're going to have to give a little to get a little."

Before, when I had said that type of thing, he had shivered and shrunk. Now he accepted it, and there was even a trace of eagerness in his voice.

"What would I have to do?"

"I'd like to put some make up on you."

"Make up." He was still, frozen, and yet this was sort of a make or break point. Oh, he would eventually do it, but I'd rather him do it now, and without the fuss. I wanted to get him past this make or break point quickly.

"You mean put make up on me. Like…like powder and cream and stuff."

I was sitting at my make up table, putting on my own make up, and I didn't look at him.

"Of course if you don't want to…" and the unsaid portion of that sentence…*if you don't want me to fuck you*…

"Well, I guess…I mean…it wouldn't hurt."

I turned to him, "Of course not, honey. Women put on make up every day, and you know why?"

He didn't say anything. I could tell deep shifts were happening in his delicate psyche.

"Because it's fun, and it feels good. You'll feel so pretty, and you'll look so good in your bra and panties."

I turned back to the mirror. "Of course if you don't want to…"

He stood silently for a full two minutes, just staring at me. I had to force myself not to suddenly look at him.

"Well, if you really want to…"

"No, no, honey. It's if you want to. If you want make up I'll help you put it on. This is all about you, honey."

He must have stood silently for a full five minutes as I finished making myself up. I was just rolling on my bright, red lipstick when he mumbled. "Sure."

"Sure, what?"

"Sure, I'd like to put on some make up."

I turned to him. "Well, okay. I'll help you, sweetie. Here, take my place."

I moved to the side and he sat down in my make up chair. He stared at the bottles and jars as if they would bite him.

"Now this is moisturizer, turn towards me a bit. Moisturizer moistens your skin, but it also cleans it. It will clean out your pores and your skin will be able to breath."

I used a small sponge to clean his face.

"This is primer. It will prepare your face, smooth it out so we can…"

I went through the steps quickly but efficiently.

He watched as his face lost color, then gained color and definition. I softened his cheekbones and his jawline. I worked on his throat, and finally I was working on his eyes.

I held a pencil next to his eyes and he was gulping. As I made the lines he was aware of how dangerous this was.

Then I shadowed his eyes, and, finally, I held up a tube of lipstick.

"Are you ready?"

"Uh, yes."

"After this you won't be a man anymore."

He stared at me.

"This is going to really make you into a woman. Are you sure you want me to paint your lips?"

"I…I…" he could hardly speak, but he managed to nod his head.

"Okay," I colored his lips, and he watched me, and was in awe. That I could do this to him, change him, change his whole idea of himself, was mind boggling.

I sat back and we stared at the mirror.

I leaned forward and picked up a hairbrush and began combing out his hair, fluffing it a bit. He had longish hair, and while it wasn't perfect, at least not yet, it was a start.

"Should I get a wig?" he asked.

"Your hair is almost long enough. A month from now we'll be giving you perms."

Another big gulp.

"Okay, I've got one other surprise for you. Stand up."

He stood up and stared at me. He was perfectly feminine. A little diet, some hormones, and he would lose the shoulders and his butt would round out.

I reached under my make up table and brought out a bag. I lifted a box out of the bag and held it out to him.

"What's this?" he sounded a little breathy. I do believe the poor boy was turning himself on.

"Open it."

He opened it, and his eyes grew large and his mouth opened.

High heels. And I couldn't wait to paint his toenails. They would look so cute peeking out under the instep strap.

"Oh, my gosh!"

"It took me a while, but I think I've got the size right. Go ahead and put them on."

He leaned over and slid his feet into the shoes, buckled the little straps, then stood up and looked down.

Oh. My. God. He was beautiful. His face was so feminine and his bra and panties so sexy, and his hair, puffed out and sprayed. And I really loved his lips. I had used plumper and gloss on them, and they were full and sexy and I wanted to kiss them in the worst way.

I stepped up to him, turned him so we could stand together in the full length mirror.

We stood, two beautiful women, and he was trembling.

"Honey, if it's all right, I think I'd like to fuck you now."

He turned to me, and the eagerness in his eyes was almost pathetic.

I went to my dresser and took out a tangle of straps and a dildo.

"Wait...what is...wait..."

I buckled the strap on around my waist and fitted the dildo into the socket.

"What are you...I didn't..."

"Honey? Tommy? I thought you understood. I said I was going to fuck you. What did you expect?"

"But...I...I..."

"Now climb up on the bed. I want you on all fours. Butt in the air."

"But...I..." he was almost crying.

"Now don't cry. I don't want you to mess your make up."

"But I—"

"Tommy!" I stamped my foot. "This is what we have been working towards. This is what you want to be. And this is the real final step. Now are you going to get on the bed? Or am I going to have to get out the paddle?"

"Paddle?"

"Paddle. If you don't get on the bed right this instant I will spank your ass until you can't sit down for a month."

If I had tried this a month previous, or even a week previous, it would have failed. But Tommy was coming around. He had lost the power to resist me, and...he liked what was happening. He might protest, but his cock was trying to become hard, and he couldn't lie about that.

Mumbling under his breath, saying I know not what, he climbed on the bed and turned his butt towards me.

I grabbed a glob of lube and moved between his legs. He jerked when I put the lube on his asshole and started rubbing it in.

"Oh, fuck..." he whispered. "Oh, fuck!"

I reamed his hole gently, making sure it was slippery, slide-y good. Then I pushed the top of my cock against his brown star.

He tensed up, became rigid.

I slapped his ass and snapped, "None of that. If you don't relax it's going to hurt. I don't want your first time to hurt!"

He forced himself to relax, and I massaged his ass and thighs and kept reaming his asshole. Finally, he was ready.

Moving very, very slowly, I pushed the tip of my dick into Tommy. He started to resist, but I kept slapping his ass and waiting, and finally we had the head in. It just sort of popped, and I had my dick inside his anus.

He was breathing hard, like he had just run a race, and I soothed him, patted his fanny, and slowly began to work in and out.

For long minutes I pushed in and out. I could feel the raised veins of my plastic peter rubbing against his anal walls. He was gasping and gulping and his ass was twitching. He was liking it, but he was still scared.

"How you doing, lover?"

"I'm…I'm okay."

"Good. I'm going to drive in a little harder. You tell me if you like it."

"Okay," his voice was a timid, little whisper.

I picked up speed, started ramming him harder and harder. He started to grunt, the he began to push back. I smiled. It wouldn't be long now.

After another minute he started soughing, breathing out in a more relaxed manner. I knew it was happening. I was pressing on his prostate and his semen was leaking out.

"How are you feeling?" I slowed down.

"Oh, man," he sighed. "I just…it's relaxing."

"You're cumming."

"What?"

"Feel your cock."

He unbalanced briefly, going to three limbs, and he reached down to feel his cage. He brought up his hand and stared at it. It had a big glob of semen on it.

"What..what is this?"

"It's your cum, lover. I told you. You're cumming."

"But I'm not having an orgasm."

"That's okay. You're getting rid of that nasty spunk. You'll be empty, really empty. I'm going to pull out now."

"Do you have to?" he begged.

"I do. We don't want to overdo it. Besides, this is not for pleasure, it's just to empty you."

I pulled out, and he groaned. Then he fell forward and just lay there and breathed.

I got up and took off my strap on. I tossed it on the floor. Tommy would wash it later and put it away. I went to the bed where he was still laying.

"Roll over. Put this mask on."

"What? Why?" But he did as I asked.

I fastened his wrists and ankles to the poles.

I unlocked his cock and...

SPROING!

"Oh! Why is it so hard?"

"Because while your balls are empty, your mind still thinks you've got a full load. You didn't get your orgasm, remember?"

"Oh."

I stared down at him and grinned. He was so fucking hot, with that female face and those juicy, red lips. And he was making me so fucking hot.

He couldn't see me, but I had my blouse open and was wearing a half bra. My nipples felt electric in the cool air.

I squatted over him and began to lower myself.

Oh, God! It felt good. I had been using the vibrator, and while that's good, it's nothing like the feel of hot, hard flesh.

He gasped as I engulfed him, and he began to thrust up into me.

I let him. This was what I wanted. I had been craving a real dicking.

I sank until he was balls deep, and I wiggled, and he groaned and I could feel his cock rubbing my insides.

"Oh, God!"

He fucked me, hard, and I let myself go a little limp. I stayed on top, but I wanted to feel that delicious feeling of giving it up.

And, finally, I started to squirt. "FU-U-UCK!" I yelled, and my pussy tensed and my pelvis locked up. I had my nipples in my hands and I gripped them so hard I was afraid they would bleed.

But it felt good, and the white hot heat swarmed me, took away my senses, and it was a long minute before I started to return to my senses.

"Okay, baby." I stood up.

"No! No!" He grasped for me, but I slapped his hands away. I looked down on him, wiggling, writhing, fucking the air and getting no where.

"Please! Please! I haven't cum!"

"And you're not going to. You have no sperm in you."

"But I'm still horny?"

"You're mind is. But your body isn't able to squirt, at least for a day or two."

I got off the bed and headed for a shower. When I got out he was still moaning and whining.

"Quiet down now," I slapped his dick.

"Ow!" but he quieted.

"Now, I can leave you here and put the tube on later, or I can go get the peas. Which would you like?

"I...can I just lay here?"

"Very well," and I started to walk out of the room, then I had a thought and I turned around.

"Tommy?"

"Yeah?" his chest was heaving as he tried to regain control of himself.

"We started down this road a while ago, and...are you bored anymore?"

"Oh, God, no!"

I smiled.

"And am I beautiful? Do you love me?"

He started to cry. "I love you...you're the most beautiful woman on earth...please...I'm sorry."

I smiled and left the room.

END

Story too short?
Didn't want it to end?
Then check out these

FULL LENGTH NOVELS!

on the following pages.
And if you want to stick with the shorts,
scroll past the novels
and you will find BIG collections
of the finest erotica in the world!
SCROLL DOWN

FULL LENGTH BOOKS!

THE classic of feminization.

Alex is ensnared by an internet stalker. Day after day he is forced to feminize. His neighbor finds out and the situation becomes worse. Now his wife is due home, and he doesn't know what to do. What's worse, he is starting to like it.

Sissy Ride: The Book!

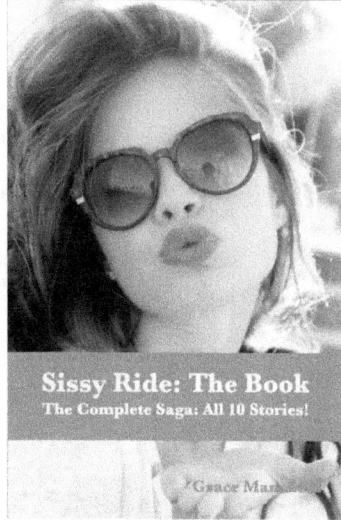

Sissy Ride: The Book
The Complete Saga: All 10 Stories!

Grace Man...

Roscoe was a power player in Hollywood. He was handsome, adored, and had one fault - he liked to play practical jokes. Now his wife is playing one on him, and it's going to be the grandest practical joke of all time.
I Changed My Husband into a Woman

Kindle customers said: Told first-person by loving but vengeful wife of rich cheating husband...Excellent read for forced-fem lovers...the deflowering was perfect.

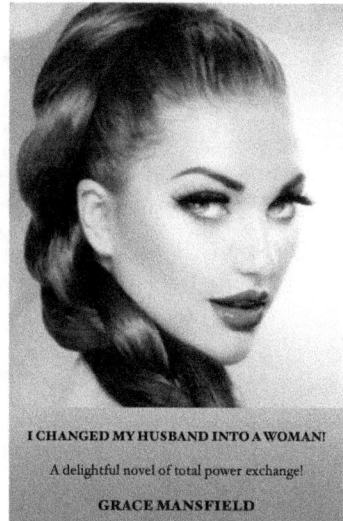

I CHANGED MY HUSBAND INTO A WOMAN!
A delightful novel of total power exchange!
GRACE MANSFIELD

FULL LENGTH BOOKS!

Randy catches his wife cheating, but a mysterious woman is about to take him in hand and teach him that when a woman cheats…it is the man's fault.

The Big Tease!

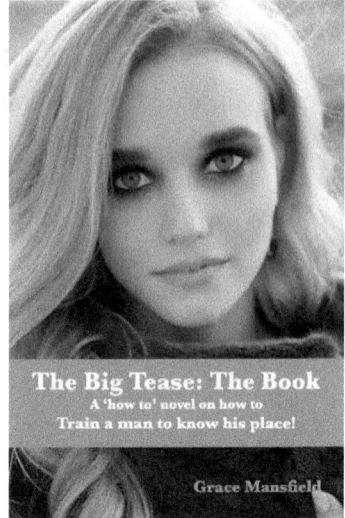

The Big Tease: The Book
A 'how to' novel on how to
Train a man to know his place!

Grace Mansfield

Sam thought he was a tough guy. He was cock of the walk, a real, live, do or die Mr. Tough Guy.

Then he made a mistake. He took on the wrong … woman.

This is the story of what happened when Sam finally met his match and learned who the really tough people are.

Too Tough to Feminize

Carol said: Ms Mansfield certainly understands the full force of female superiority and empowerment !

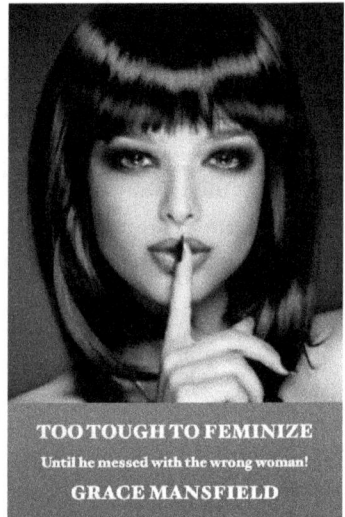

TOO TOUGH TO FEMINIZE
Until he messed with the wrong woman!
GRACE MANSFIELD

I felt myself surrendering to the 'woman in me', and wanting to be a part of a dynamic woman's world.

FULL LENGTH BOOKS!

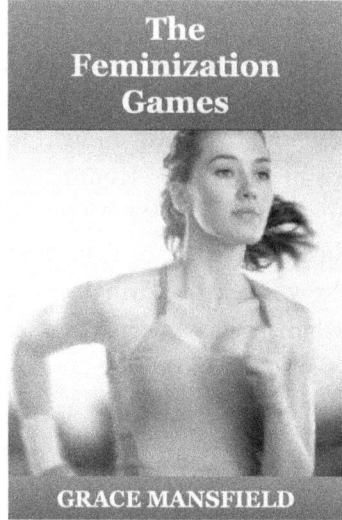

The
Feminization
Games

GRACE MANSFIELD

Jim Camden was a manly man, until the day he crossed his wife. Now he's in for a battle of the sexes, and if he loses…he has to dress like a woman for a week. But what he doesn't know is the depths of manipulation his wife will go to. Lois Camden, you see, is a woman about to break free, and if she has to step on her husband to do it…so be it. And Jim is about to learn that a woman unleashed is a man consumed.

The Feminization Games

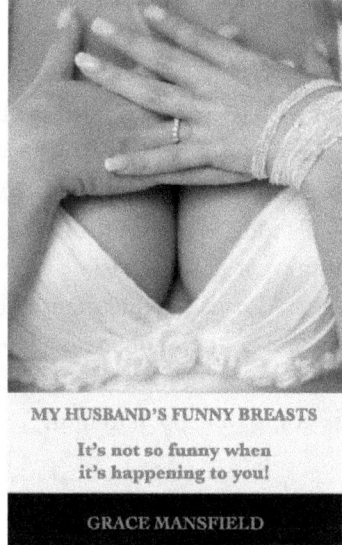

MY HUSBAND'S FUNNY BREASTS

It's not so funny when
it's happening to you!

GRACE MANSFIELD

Tom Dickson was a happy camper. He lived a good life, had a beautiful wife, then he started to grow breasts, his hair grew long, and his body reshaped. Now Tom is on the way to being a woman, and he doesn't know why.

My Husband's Funny Breasts

FULL LENGTH BOOKS!

Rick Boston and his beautiful wife, Jamey, move to Stepforth Valley, where Rick is offered a job at a high tech cosmetics company. The House of Chimera is planning on releasing a male cosmetics line, and Rick is their first test subject. Now Rick is changing. The House of Chimera has a deep, dark secret, and Rick is just one more step on the path to world domination!

The Stepforth Husband

Grace Mansfield

<u>The Stepforth Husband</u>

Robert said: I was expecting less and got more! Having knowledge of the original story I made some assumptions. Intricate emotions and some a few twists later and Ms Mansfield has a good book on her hands.

Alex has to live in an old, decrepit mansion for the summer. Worse, he's supposed to follow the directions of an old biddy who, right off the bat, makes him wear girl clothes!

Alex is in for a surprise, however, because the house is haunted, and wearing girl clothes is the least of what is going to happen to him!

Feminized by a Ghost

Grace Mansfield

<u>Feminized by a Ghost</u>

FULL LENGTH BOOKS!

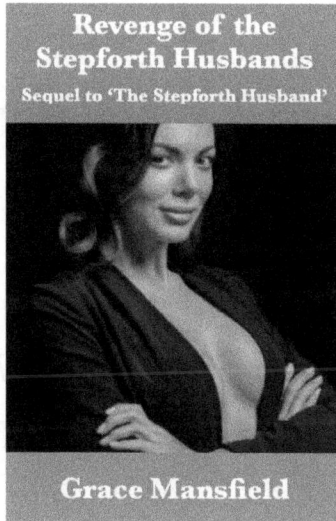

This is the second book in the Stepforth Series. The first book is 'The Stepforth Husband.'

Judd is the product of the Amazons. the Amazons are an ancient race of women who are working for the betterment of mankind.

Judd must go to Stepforth Valley and uncover an insidious plot to make the men of the world into women. He will be chemically changed, betrayed by those who love him, and, in the end, come to the truth of the world.

Revenge of the Stepforth Husbands

A Kindle Customer said of The Stepforth Husband and the Revenge of the Stepforth Husbands: This two book set is an intriguing blending of erotica, adventure, mystery and philosophy. Sated you will be regarding the first three categories and if your world or life views can accept it, be intrigued by the author's theological speculations as described at the end of the second book. Fiction is always made more interesting when it is based in truth.

There are MORE full length novels at:

GROPPER PRESS

BUT…
if you want save money
check out the following link…
Big Erotic Collections!

You'll find massive collections
of the finest erotica in the world!
Just like the ones on the following pages.

BIG COLLECTIONS!

Save money
SEVEN sexy stories
A sorority that feminizes...'Tootsie'
goes all the way...National lipstick
day and all the men in Hollywood start
growing breasts...learning to be a man
by being a woman, and more, more,
more.

The Electric Groin!

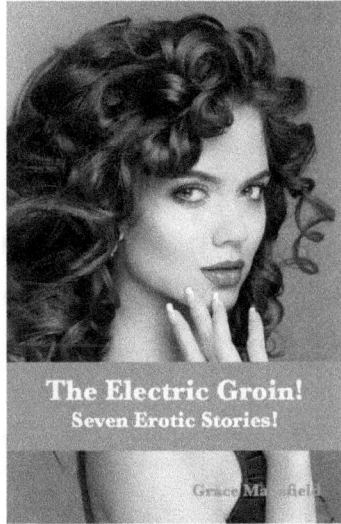

The Electric Groin!
Seven Erotic Stories!

Grace Mansfield

Save money with SEVEN erotic
stories
Men turning into women because of the
vaccine...a woman makes her husband
wear a chastity device, then they swap
bodies...feminization training...
feminized by his sister...and more,
more!

Quivering Buns

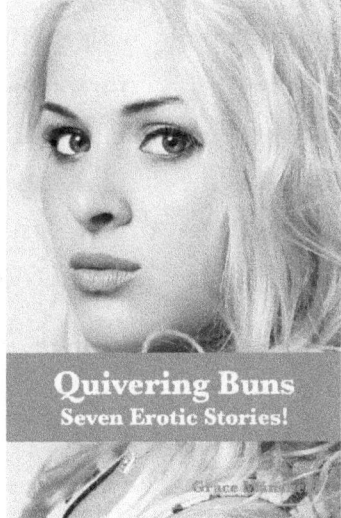

Quivering Buns
Seven Erotic Stories!

Grace Mansfield

BIG COLLECTIONS!

Save money with SEVEN sexy stories

A sorority that feminizes, 'Tootsie' goes all the way, National lipstick day and all the men in Hollywood start growing breasts, learning to be a man by being a woman, and more, more, more.

The Shivering Bone!

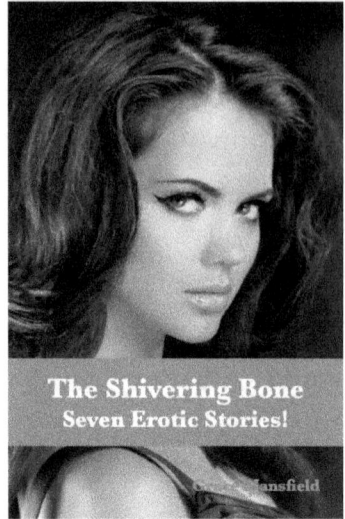

The Shivering Bone
Seven Erotic Stories!

Save money with SEVEN erotic stories

A nephew changed into a girl... emasculating a cheating husband...a feminized cop...sentenced to feminization...and a LOT More!

Stories to Pump your Heart

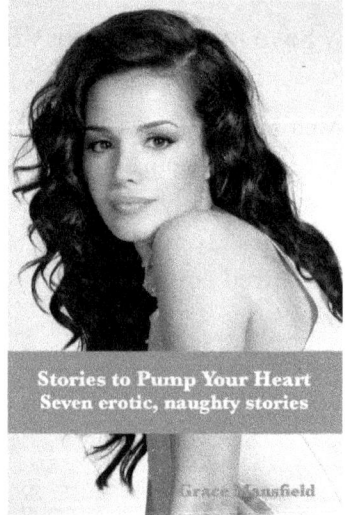

Stories to Pump Your Heart
Seven erotic, naughty stories

BIG COLLECTIONS!

Save money with SEVEN erotic stories

His penis grows longer when he cheats!...mad scientist changes man into woman!...a man has to learnto be a female model...and much, MUCH more!

The Whisper of Flesh

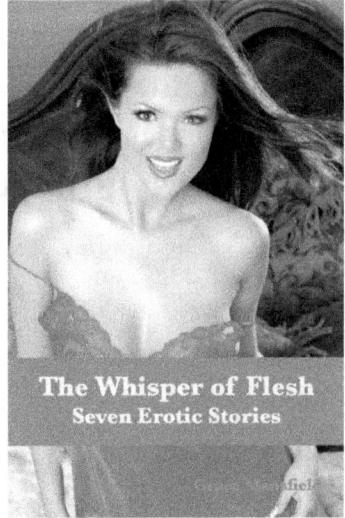

The Whisper of Flesh
Seven Erotic Stories

Save money with FIVE erotic stories

A horn dog is feminized...a husband learns about sissyhood...a friendly party becomes an intense sexual competition...12 men play a game, and one of them is a woman ...and much, MUCH more!

Skin Games!

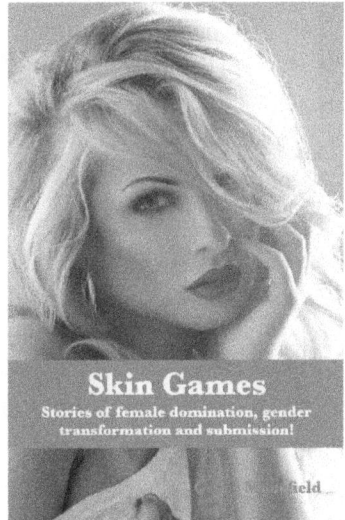

Skin Games
Stories of female domination, gender transformation and submission!

CHECK IT OUT!

Here are 99 hot and steamy stories! Feminization, female domination, BDSM, male chastity…check out the titles and find one you think might be interesting! And there are more at:

https://gropperpress.wordpress.com

The Bank Robber Became a Lady
I Gave My Man Boobs
The Day the Democrats Turned the Republicans into Girls
The Lactating Man
The Sexual Edge
My Neighbor Feminized Me
COVID Feminized My Husband
Revenge of the Lactating Babes
The Were-Fem
I Was Feminized by the FBI
The Feminist Experiment
We Made Him Our Fem Boy
A Witch Feminized Me
9 to 5 Feminism
The Half and Half Man
The Feminine Vaccination
The Great Gender Revolt
Big Femme
League of Lactators
The Sexual Matrix
I Changed My Nephew into a Girl
How to Emasculate Your Cheating Husband
Feminized for Granny
Feminized in 100 Days
Feminized Cop
The Sissy Ride
Sentenced to Feminization
Feminization is in My DNA

Feminization Resources
Body Swapping with Chastity
I've Got to Have It
Feminized by My Sister
Feminization of a Salesman
Feminization By Act of Congress
A Man Caught
The Lactating Woman
Listening to Sex
The Feminization Curse
The Man Who Would Be Woman
Feminized by Neuralink
My Wife Dominated Me
Dominated By a Gang of Women
My Wife Made Me Worship Her
He Wanted a Real Chest
Forced to be a Crossdresser
Cheating is Forbidden
The Feminization of Jackson
How to Make Your Husband into a Sissy Slave
Feminization Makes a Whole Man
A Woman Again
I Rule My Man
A Month of Feminization
A Sorority Feminized Me
Being a Woman
Made into a Woman
National Lipstick Day
Sexual Borders
The Intersex Man
Self Respect Through Feminization
The Pinocchio Condition
Racing for a Woman
The Great Gender Transformation Conspiracy
To Sacrifice for Love
Feminized by a Neighbor Lady
My Husband the Model

The Party in the Bedroom
The Cure for Limp
I Inherited Being a Woman
Jessie's Boobs
He Wanted It Tighter
She Wanted It Bigger
Subliminal Feminization
Boob Maximizer
He Was a Female Model
The Politics of Feminization
My Husband Became a Pole Dancer
Mystery Boobs
More Woman Than Man
The Feminization Corps
She Transgendered Me
The Sex Games
Feminization 101
Feminizing the Horn Dog
My Husband is a Sissy
My Husband the Girl
Satan's Panties
The Picture of Femian Grey
My Mother's Panties
The Ladies' Sissy Society
We Feminized a Burglar
Horn Dog Comeuppance
The Ultimate Erotic Fantasy
The Church of Feminization
Oops!
I Feminized a Reporter
The Gender Transformation Club
Emergency Transition
I Made Him My Sissy Slave
Emasculation Made Easy

https://gropperpress.wordpress.com

If you liked
'A Chest Full of Surprises!'
you will really love…

'I Changed My Husband into a Woman'

A full length novel by Grace Mansfield

Here is an excerpt…

"What the fuck!"

I roused myself from a deep and very deserved sleep, only to see Roscoe standing next to the bed, looking down at his feet and cursing.

"Wha…" I mumbled, pulling the covers over me and trying to look like I was still asleep. In truth, though I was tired, I was as awake as I had ever been.

"Did you do this?" His voice was going up. "Is this your idea of a joke?"

"Shut up," I whined. "I wanna sleep!"

"No! Wake up! Why'd you do this?"

"Do what?" and I finally rolled over and made my eyes sleepy and tired.

Oh, baby, was I acting. And I was acting in front of the fellow who had created a half a dozen Best Actor Oscar winners. This was going to take all my prowess to pull off.

"My toes! Look at my toes."

I blinked, and edged towards the side of the bed so I could look down to where he was pointing. And I exulted. He had felt he had to explain that it was his toes, so he was just working off emotion and blaming whoever was closest. He didn't have any clue as to why his toes were red.

"What the fuck!" I opened my eyes wide and stared at his tootsies.

"Why'd you do this?"

I looked up at him and put a tiny edge of anger in my voice. "I didn't do that! Why the hell would I paint my sissy husband's toes red?" Very important to get the word sissy into the conversation as quickly as possible. "Do I look like I'm the kind of girl who'd marry a sissy?"

He kept trying to look fierce, but I could tell that my arrows had hit the mark. In some odd, almost invisible way he shriveled. He withdrew slightly into himself. I had met the challenge and acted my way out of being the culprit.

"Okay, okay," then he tried again. "You did this because I jacked off on you the other day."

"First, I just said I didn't do that!" I pointed at his toes. "And, I already got you back, and, husband of mine, practical jokes aren't my forte." At least they usually weren't. I was enjoying this; I was thinking of a career change. Sandy Tannenbaum, Practical Joker Extraordinaire!

"So who did this?"

Now I looked at him suspiciously. "There's only two people in this room."

He sputtered in outrage, so I kept up the attack. "So why did you paint your toe nails red?"

"I didn't!"

"There's nobody else here!" I was pushing him now. I had been accused unfairly (he thought) so I had to act the outrage. I narrowed my eyes. "Are you going pervert on me?"

"I didn't do this!" he wailed.

"Well I didn't, and I didn't figure on waking up next to Bruce Jenner."

Oh, Jesus!" he almost ran to my make up station and started looking for polish remover. "Where is it!?"

I got out of bed, and went to him. I didn't want him making a mess, so I handed him a bottle of polish remover. He grabbed at it like a sailor grabs a life preserver after jumping off the Titanic. He sat down and lifted his foot up to the edge of the chair.

"Hold on," I said. I took the remover out of his hands. "I don't want you making a mess. Come here."

I led him into the bathroom. "Put your foot here," I pointed to the john. He placed his foot on the toilet and I sat cross legged in front of it. I giggled.

"What?" he groused.

"It is sort of cute. Hubbie gives himself a peddie. Make a good TV series."

He let his breath out in disgust. "I'm a man's man, not a girly man."

Yeah, that's right, you like to get young girl's pregnant. how manly. But I didn't say that, I just thought it, and kept manipulating him.

"Well, you might say so, but Roscoe Junior says otherwise."

Now, truth, he wasn't really all that hard, just sort of a morning half woodie, but I reached up and grabbed his meat and in a second he was throbbing in my hand.

"Hey!" he said. But he wasn't really protesting. What man would object to a pair of sexy hands fondling his man pole? "Take the polish off."

"Oh, okay." but the damage was done. He was now erect, and associating that erection with nail polish. Manly man. Huh!

So I hummed a tune and stripped the polish off and returned his toes to their 'manly' state.

"Okay," he said. Standing and looking down at his repaired manhood, uh, nails.

"Not even a thanks?"

"Thank you," and he did sound abashed. "But I have no idea how… somebody must have broken in and done it."

"While you slept? They painted your nails and you didn't even wake up?"

"Well, I was pretty drunk."

I'll say.

"Not that drunk," I lied. "You never get that drunk."

"Well, yeah. But somebody did it." We left the bathroom then and re-entered the bedroom. He walked over to the double windows, which led out to a small patio. He tried the doors. "See! they're open!"

"We're on the second floor."

"He had a ladder."

"He?"

"Well, you don't think a woman did this?"

"Those nails were done pretty well. Men don't know how to apply polish that well." Then I cocked my head and it was obvious what I was thinking.

"Don't look at me that way! I didn't polish my own nails."

I shrugged. "Okay. So Spiderman left off fighting crime for one day so he could paint your nails."

He made a grimace.

"Or maybe somebody just walked in because our door is unlocked." I swung the bedroom door opened.

"Well, I don't…"

"Forget it, Roscoe." I use his name when I am angry with him, or irritated, and he took notice of that. "just admit that you did some sleep walking." Then I giggled, "Or sleep toenail painting."

"Oh, shut up." he brushed past me and headed down the stairs. It was a mark of how irritated and upset he was that he had forgotten to get dressed.

"Ahem!" I cleared my throat.

He turned at the top of the stairs and looked at me. Oh, the look on his face. Irritated, confused. Priceless.

I looked at his groin, placed an elbow in a palm and wiggled my index finger in the air.

He looked down at himself, mumbled a curse word I dasn't dare repeat, and stomped back into the bedroom.

This has been an excerpt from

I Changed My Husband into a Woman!
Read it on kindle or paperback